BACK ROAD MYSTERIES
BOOK THREE
THE POND

JIMMY ZEIGLER

Copyright © 2024 Jimmy Zeigler

All Rights Reserved

ISBN:

Contents

Dedication i

Acknowledgment ii

About the Author iii

Chapter One 1

Chapter Two 9

Chapter Three 15

Chapter Four 20

Chapter Five 27

Chapter Six 31

Chapter Seven 41

Chapter Eight 53

Chapter Nine 58

Chapter Ten 65

Chapter Eleven 79

Chapter Twelve 85

Chapter Thirteen 95

Chapter Fourteen 105

Chapter Fifteen 113

Chapter Sixteen 121

Chapter Seventeen 126

Chapter Eighteen 132

Chapter Nineteen 136

Dedication

To my L. A. Fitness buddy, Gary Pagano, my best fan. He has purchased all of my books, I only hope he reads them!!

Acknowledgment

Writers of US for the help in constructing my book and cover. Brad Haizlip for my UTube Interview. My wife for her help in proofreading and a Thank You to all the nice people who buy this book. Special thank you to Mike Carper for selling all my books in his two stores located in New Castle, Va.

About the Author

The Author of The Jimmy Zeigler Novels, J. F. Zimmerman, is pleased to present you with his Third Novel of the series of Seven, called Back Road Mysteries-Book Three-The Pond. The first The Church has been out for some time now and the second, The Tower is about to go on line for sale. He hopes you will enjoy the continued story of Clifford and Janet and their Murder Solving abilities.

This Novel begins where The Back Road Mysteries, The Tower left off. Janet and Clifford were getting married in the last book. They are about to become parents of twins and later another son in this book and Clifford has to deal with two murders where the bodies are found in a watershed pond and a cavern. This takes place in the little County of Craig, in the State of Virginia, located in the USA.

Chapter One

Clifford and Janet had been married for a couple of years, and all was well with them. They had been married about six months when she thought she was pregnant, but it turned out to be a false alarm. They were sad when she wasn't, but Cliff just told her not to worry, when the time was right, she would be. She had not been able to get pregnant as they planned, but they were still working on it.

Clifford didn't seem to be excited about the situation; he just kept on saying, Honey, when it is time, you will become a Mama. You need to relax and enjoy the ride and of course, after he had made the statement, he wanted to make love. She knew he was right, but she couldn't be as relaxed about it as he was.

The lovemaking was great; it had always been great from the start, so she just couldn't understand why she couldn't conceive. "Oh well," she thought, "one of these days, hopefully, I will." Cliff came in the door just as she was having these thoughts.

"Hey, woman, how would you like to go for a ride up Dick's Creek? I heard the other day that they might have to drain at least one of the ponds up there. Something about the Corps of Engineers being afraid it might burst and flood Dick's Creek Valley. Both ponds are large, and if either burst, it would create a real mess up in the Valley."

"Sure, bud, give me a minute to finish what I've started here, and we can hit the road."

Clifford went over and took his seat in his chair because he'd been married long enough to know not to get in a hurry. He picked up the book he'd been reading and flipped it open to the page where he had stopped. It was a murder mystery; he loved reading them. It was amazing how true to life some of them were written.

They jumped into their new Ford F-150, which they had just bought; the old truck had given up the ghost a couple of weeks ago. The truck had been a good vehicle; his father had purchased it new in 1973 and put a hundred thousand miles on it before Cliff started driving it.

When it died, Cliff had a total of three hundred thousand miles on it. They went and purchased a new one and had the junkyard come and haul the old one away. Cliff and Janet had gone to the Ford dealership in Roanoke the day old Betsy died to see what they had on the lot. Old Betsy was light blue with a white top—nothing fancy, just rubber mats and vinyl seat covers. That was what they wanted to buy now, but guess what? There's no such thing anymore.

All the new trucks had carpet and leather seats—or at least that's all they found on the lot. They did find one with a baby blue bottom and a white top. It had a lot more luxury options, but they decided they could live with them; at least they got the color they wanted. There were prettier trucks on the lot, but Cliff wanted it to be the color of the old truck he'd driven for so long.

He had read two chapters of his book before Janet came out of the bedroom and down the hall to join him.

"You ready, my dear?" he asked with a smile on his face.

"Yep, but if it's too soon, I can go back into the bedroom and stay a little while longer," she replied.

They went out to their new truck and started driving west on Route 42. Their plan was to drive over the crooked road that led from Sinking Creek Valley to Johns Creek Valley. It was a winding little road, but if you went slow and kept to the right when going around the sharp turns, you could drive it safely. It was the idiots who refused to slow down and stay to the right that sometimes caused wrecks on Wagon Trail Road. Route 42 was somewhat curvy, but the lanes were wide, and you could do the speed limit on most of it.

Once you started on the little road across the mountain to Johns Creek, you had to slow to thirty-five mph. If you didn't slow down, you were very likely to have a head-on crash with someone driving too fast like yourself.

"Well, my sweet, here we go," Cliff said to her. "Hold on to your overhead handle, just in case I meet someone on our side of the road and have to head toward the ditch to avoid a crash."

She reached up and caught hold of the strap above her door window. No sooner had she grabbed hold of the strap than he started into one of the hairpin curves, and sure enough, about halfway through the curve, they met a car on their side of the road.

Cliff braked and steered as far to his side as he could without putting his new truck in the ditch. They missed hitting the other truck by just an inch or two. He looked at her and asked, "You okay, honey?"

"Right as rain," she replied.

"Now, that's an old country saying," Cliff commented with a smile.

They were almost off the mountain now and hadn't encountered any more vehicles, much to Janet's relief. The one close call had nearly made her pee her pants. Once off the mountain, they entered a valley of rolling green hills with purple mountains in the background. She thought the valley looked as if time had passed it by, and God had kept it pristine.

It took them about five minutes to reach the crossroads where a small one-room country store was located.

"Janet, have you ever been in this little store?"

"No, I've never stopped in."

With that, he pulled into the gravel parking lot and declared, "We're here!"

They went into the store, and the new owner greeted them with a, "Hey, how are things going?"

Clifford answered, "Just fine. My wife hasn't been in this store, so we stopped by so she could look around and see if there's anything she might want."

"Well, help yourself. I'll be over here if you need any help," she said. The woman walked with a cane, but she made her way to a chair behind the counter and took a seat.

"Look around, Janet. I'll go over and chat with the owner while you shop."

"Okay, I already see some interesting things on the shelves."

Clifford walked over to the lady and introduced himself.

"Glad to meet you. I'm Mary Mann. I just bought the store from the Huffman family. I needed something to keep me busy. I own a home in the Black Diamond Estates down the road, so this little store is convenient for me to come and go. I have one of the local guys stocking the shelves, but I love to come over here and chat with my customers."

They chatted while Janet shopped. She came over to the cash register counter holding several items, including a homemade quilt for only forty dollars, which was a steal at that price, and a few other small things. She was a happy camper now that she'd found these goodies at such low prices.

Clifford had learned a bit about Mary while Janet was shopping. She was a widow who had moved from Ohio to Craig County. Her son had gone to Virginia Tech, and while visiting him, she had seen an advertisement for land for sale at Black Diamond Farm. She decided to move to a somewhat warmer climate and bought a two-acre lot where she had a house built. She had four children—three boys, one of whom lived in Blacksburg nearby, while the other two were in Ohio, just outside of Cleveland. She also had a daughter but wasn't sure where she was at the moment. Mary seemed nice, but Clifford couldn't understand why she would move away from two children to be closer to one.

They got back into the truck and started down the road. It took five minutes to reach the bridge where Johns Creek Road met Dick's Creek Road. They pulled up to the stop sign and could see the Johns Creek Christian Church almost in front of them. Cliff took a left turn and headed down what was called Dick's Creek. The ponds were supposed to be a couple of miles down this road, or so he thought. After driving a few miles, he realised he didn't know where the ponds were. He turned around and went back to the little store.

"Mary, I'm not as smart as I thought I was. Where can I find the watershed ponds? I thought they were on Dick's Creek, but I couldn't find them."

She just smiled at him. "Dear boy, you went the wrong direction. Go west on the road in front of the store, and about a mile up, you'll see a dirt road. Turn right and follow it up to the ponds."

It took them about five minutes to reach the road and another five to slowly climb the rough road up to the ponds. The watershed ponds were designed to catch runoff water from the mountains in the spring. There were all kinds of springs feeding a small branch that came off the mountain, and when the snow melted in the spring, a lot of water flowed down the mountainside from that small branch, which turned into a large stream. They pulled up to the ponds, got out of the truck, and walked over to the first one. There were danger signs warning people not to go near them, but you know people—they did anyway.

They took a stroll around the pond, but Clifford couldn't see any cracks in the dirt mound that held the water in the pond. He could tell it was deep by the colour of the water, a deep blue-green. No matter how hard you looked, you couldn't see the bottom anywhere. He guessed by the mound of dirt that it was somewhere around twenty feet deep. Depending on the snow depth on the mountain, they would let water out of the ponds in the spring to make room for the new runoff.

They both agreed that they couldn't see any reason why these ponds should be pumped dry. The dirt dykes seemed fine, but then again, they weren't engineers—so what did they know?

Getting back into the truck, they slowly made their way down the dirt road and took a left onto the main road that passed by the store. At the stop sign, they turned left onto Dick's Creek Road. This road would eventually circle back into Johns Creek Road, leading them to Route 311 and then into New Castle. When they reached the main road, they decided to head to Pine Top Restaurant for some lunch. It took them another twenty minutes to get there.

As Cliff pulled into the restaurant parking lot, he noticed a county cruiser parked there. The number twelve on the side of the car told him that Ike was inside. When they entered the building, Cliff saw his deputy eating alone in one of the booths. They walked over and asked if he'd like some company. Ike nodded yes between bites of his hamburger, and they took their seats just as the server approached.

"What can I get you two to drink?" she asked.

"Black coffee for me and water with lemon for her, please," Cliff replied.

The server left to get their drink order after giving them menus and silverware.

"Is this supper, Cliff?" Janet asked. "If so, I need to go big. If not, I'll eat light."

"It's Lupper, dear—after lunch but before supper."

"I guess that means I'd better go big, then."

The server returned, and Janet ordered the Meatloaf Special, which came with mashed potatoes, slaw, and pinto beans. Cliff ordered the same; it sounded good to him when Janet ordered hers. Ike was having a late lunch because he had to work an extra couple of hours due to another deputy coming in late for the second shift. Ike had retired a couple of years ago but didn't enjoy being at home, so Cliff hired him back part-time, and it was working out well.

They enjoyed a pleasant time with Ike, and the Lupper hit the spot. A few more of their friends came in, and they spent some time chatting with them before saying their goodbyes and heading up the mountain to their house.

As they started up the road, Janet moved closer to Cliff, loving the feeling of contentment she felt when she was near him. The past two years had been blissful for them—or at least for her. She had discovered that he could be hard to read at times, having been somewhat of a loner before they married. But she loved him just the way he was and wouldn't trade him for anything.

When they arrived home, they went straight to their bedroom. Her warm head resting on his shoulder had aroused him, and she could tell by the front of his trousers. She was in the mood for some late-afternoon loving too.

Chapter Two

The next morning, Janet woke up to find Cliff already up and eager for a morning romp. Although she wasn't feeling her best, she decided to go along with it, thinking she could still help him out. As they started making love, she found herself feeling better and ended up enjoying the experience as much as he did. However, after they finished, she noticed something different, a feeling she couldn't quite place.

For the next two weeks, Janet felt unusually energetic and full of life. But by the third week, things took a turn. She began feeling sick every morning, and the smell of coffee brewing made her nauseous. She switched to drinking water or milk instead of her usual coffee, which puzzled Cliff.

By the end of that third week, Janet had a suspicion about what was happening. During a shopping trip to Roanoke, she picked up a pregnancy test. As soon as she got home, she took the test, and when it turned blue, she realized she was going to be a mother, likely in about eight months.

She spent the entire afternoon filled with joy, barely able to resist the urge to call Cliff at work and share the news. However, as the hour for Cliff's return approached, doubts began to creep in. What if the test was wrong, like it had been last time? But then she reassured herself, remembering that she hadn't experienced the same nausea and symptoms before. To be certain, she called her doctor and scheduled an appointment for the following week, deciding to wait until then to tell Cliff.

When Cliff came home, he greeted her with a kiss on the back of her neck before heading to the bathroom for a shower. As the hot water worked its magic on his tired muscles, he heard the shower door unlatch. Turning around with a smile, he knew what was about to happen. Janet joined him in the shower, already naked and ready for some loving. They made love under the cascading water, and afterward, Janet felt even more certain that she was pregnant, just from the way their bodies connected.

Once they dried off and stepped out of the shower, she gave him a gentle, sweet kiss and finally told him that he was going to be a daddy. She explained that she was confident in her body's signals but had made an appointment to confirm it the next week. Cliff grinned at her and said he had also sensed she was pregnant, just from the way she felt during their lovemaking. He then gave her a kiss so passionate that it would have knocked her socks off—if she had been wearing any.

After dressing, Janet returned to the kitchen to finish making dinner. She had baked potatoes kept warm in the oven and fried chicken covered on the stovetop. She set everything on the kitchen table, and they sat down to eat. That night, feeling content and tired from the day's events, they turned in early, falling asleep as soon as their heads hit the pillows.

The next morning, Janet was jolted awake by the sound of the alarm clock. Instead of her usual routine of heading straight to the kitchen to brew coffee, she found herself rushing to the bathroom, where morning sickness had taken hold again. Clifford, hearing her retching, got up and followed her, grabbing a clean washcloth, wetting it with cold water, and handing it to her. After making sure she was alright, he went to the kitchen and started the coffee, hoping the smell wouldn't worsen her nausea. When she finally joined him in the kitchen, she looked a bit pale, but the coffee aroma didn't seem to bother her as much this time.

"So, Janet, what day next week is your doctor's appointment?" Cliff asked as he handed her a glass of water.

"Tuesday at ten a.m.," she replied.

"Alright," he said, nodding. "I'll take the day off and go with you for moral support."

Before they knew it, the following Tuesday arrived. Clifford had kept his promise and taken the day off. Janet's morning sickness had eased somewhat by then, much to her relief. They climbed into their truck and set off for Roanoke, the drive taking about an hour and twenty minutes. As they pulled into the doctor's office parking lot, Janet's anxiety started to build, and by the time they walked inside, she felt on the verge of tears.

Cliff, sensing her distress, put his arm around her and gave her a reassuring hug. "Don't worry, everything is as it should be. You're going to be a great mom. I can't wait to tell your parents. Your dad will be over the moon—he's been quietly waiting to become a granddad."

Janet smiled weakly and nodded, feeling a bit more at ease as they checked in. She was called back by the nurse right on time, leaving Clifford in the waiting room. He glanced at his watch as the minutes ticked by, growing increasingly anxious as nearly an hour passed without any sign of her. Finally, Janet and the nurse appeared in the hallway. Clifford stood up, trying to read her expression, but she gave nothing away.

"Come on, tell me, don't keep me guessing!" he urged as she

approached.

"Well," she began with a slight grin, "it's official. I'm definitely pregnant. You're going to be a daddy! From my calculations, we've got about eight months until the baby arrives."

Cliff's face lit up with joy. He gently hugged her, but she teased him, "Come on now, I'm pregnant, not made of glass. I can still handle a good hug!"

Laughing, Cliff scooped her up into a bear hug, lifting her off the ground. "We need to celebrate," he said, his excitement palpable. "Lunch it is!"

They decided to head to Paul's, a cozy restaurant in downtown Roanoke that Cliff had visited before. The restaurant was known for its lasagna, which Cliff eagerly recommended. "Janet, you've got to try the lasagna. It's to die for!"

When the server arrived, they ordered the lasagna special, along with salads and garlic bread. As they waited, they discussed the doctor's visit. Janet shared the details: the doctor had confirmed her pregnancy, everything seemed normal, but there was a slight concern. Her blood pressure had been higher than usual, 180/95 instead of her usual 130/80. The doctor advised her to monitor it daily and take things a bit easier.

Their meals arrived, and Janet, feeling unexpectedly ravenous, dug into her lasagna with gusto. Cliff chuckled, "Hey, slow down! I want to enjoy mine too."

Janet smiled, realizing he was right, and slowed her pace. They savored their meal, and afterward, Cliff paid the bill, leaving a generous thirty percent tip for the excellent service. Feeling elated by the news of impending fatherhood, he couldn't help but spread the joy.

As they walked back to their truck, Cliff asked, "Anywhere else you want to stop before we head home?"

"Yes, I need to pick up something for my morning sickness at CVS," Janet replied.

They took the Hershberger Road exit to reach the nearest CVS. Cliff stayed in the truck while Janet went inside. He had parked near the entrance and was about to doze off when the sharp sound of gunshots shattered the afternoon calm. Cliff bolted upright, heart racing, and watched in horror as two masked men burst out of the store, jumped into a car parked in the fire zone, and sped off. His police instincts kicked in, and he quickly noted the make of the car and its license plate number before rushing into the store to check on Janet.

He was relieved to see her coming out of the pharmacy area, seemingly unaware of the chaos that had just unfolded. "I thought you were going to wait in the car," she said, surprised to see him.

"I was, but I heard gunshots and got worried," he explained, still on high alert. "There were robbers. They just ran out of the store."

Janet looked confused. "Robbers? I didn't hear anything. I was at the pharmacy the whole time."

"Well, as long as you're okay," Cliff said, his relief evident. "I need to report this to the police."

Outside, the police had already arrived. Cliff approached them, identifying himself and providing a detailed description of the suspects, their car, and the license plate number. The officers were impressed by how much information he had retained in just a few seconds. After thanking him, they assured him they'd follow up if needed.

With the excitement behind them, Cliff and Janet finally headed home. The day had been eventful, to say the least, but nothing could dampen the happiness of knowing they were about to become parents.

Chapter Three

The next morning, as the alarm went off, Janet felt well enough to slide out of bed. She headed to the kitchen to put on the coffee and get their day started. Cliff woke up at the same time, but when he saw Janet get up, he decided to stay in bed a little longer. After she was out of the room, he slid out of bed and went into the bathroom. A hot shower was just what he needed to wake up his tired back and sleepy eyes.

Once he was dressed, Cliff headed down the hall to the kitchen. The hallway in their new house wasn't as long as the one in their old place, so the smell of coffee hit his nose even while he was in the shower. He walked straight to the coffee maker, poured himself a mug, and then sat down at the table. Janet was already there, nursing a cup of coffee, looking as though she was still half asleep.

"Hey, you awake, Janet?" Cliff asked, his voice soft and teasing.

She moaned a little, answering with a soft "Yes. Give me a minute, and I'll fix you some breakfast."

"You look sort of out of it this morning, hon. I can get breakfast at Pine Top this morning."

"Could you? I would appreciate that," she replied, clearly relieved.

Cliff finished his coffee, leaned over to give her a peck on the top of her head, and told her to go back to bed. He couldn't help but smile as he left the house and got into his cruiser, heading down the mountain toward his office.

It only took him about fifteen minutes to reach Pine Top Restaurant. As he walked through the door, he noticed it was unusually crowded. When the server came over to take his order, he asked her why there was such a large crowd that morning.

"There's a meeting of the Board of Supervisors this morning about the ponds up on Johns Creek," she explained. "The Army Corps of Engineers said at least one of them will have to be drained and repaired. The locals are up in arms about it."

"Oh, I see," Cliff replied. "I guess I'll have to attend the board meeting this morning. What time does it start?"

"I think at eleven a.m.," the server said.

"Thanks. I'll have an order of sausage gravy and biscuits this morning, please."

"Sure, Cliff, I'll be right back with it."

The server quickly returned with his breakfast, and Cliff dug in, savoring every bite. After finishing, he left a tip on the table and paid his bill at the cash register. He recognized some of the faces in the restaurant, but there were quite a few people he didn't know.

After breakfast, Cliff headed to his office to start his day. He set the alarm on his watch for 10:45 a.m. so he wouldn't be late for the meeting. As he went through the wanted and missing posters on his desk, he came across the one for Carla Warren again. She had been reported missing by her parents two years ago when she was supposed to catch a plane to California to visit them. Her husband claimed she had gotten on the plane, but they never heard from her again. The name "Warren" kept gnawing at Clifford, but he couldn't quite place it.

His phone alarm went off, interrupting his thoughts, and he headed to the Town Hall for the Board of Supervisors meeting. The meeting room was packed, but he managed to find a spot to stand in the back. The Chairman started the meeting by leading everyone in reciting the Pledge of Allegiance. Most of the people placed their hands over their hearts, but a few refused, standing like stone monuments instead. Cliff, as an elected officer, couldn't say anything, but he couldn't help but personally dislike those who showed such disrespect.

The board finally got to the issue of the ponds, but barely a word was spoken before a man stood up and started shouting obscenities at the Chairman. Cliff quickly walked over to the man, getting in his face.

"Sir, you need to handle yourself in an orderly fashion, or you'll have to leave this meeting," Cliff warned.

The man glared at Cliff and challenged, "Who's going to make me?"

Without hesitation, Cliff reached out, grabbed the man by the neck, and applied pressure at just the right points. The man went along with him without further resistance. Cliff arrested him for disturbing the peace and threatening a police officer, which meant he missed the rest of the meeting. The man would now have to face a judge and explain his behavior. Cliff reflected on how a lack of control over one's tongue could lead to serious trouble, especially when it infringes on the rights of others.

After dealing with the situation, Cliff needed to find out what had been decided about the ponds. He called the Chairman of the Board of Supervisors, who picked up right away.

"This is Clifford. What was decided about the ponds on Johns Creek?" Cliff asked.

"We don't have any say in the matter," the Chairman replied. "They were built by the Army Corps of Engineers and later given to the county. The county then sold them to individuals, but the Corps is still responsible for their upkeep since they're part of a watershed project. It looks like they'll start draining the larger pond next month to inspect the walls and determine what repairs are needed to prevent them from bursting."

"Thanks, I appreciate the update. I may need to keep a deputy on duty up at the ponds to keep an eye on things."

"That's probably a good idea, Cliff," the Chairman agreed.

Cliff had just hung up the phone when it rang again. He picked it up and answered, "This is Clifford Davidson, Sheriff of Craig County. How can I help you?"

Clifford thanked Sheila and walked back to his office, feeling the crisp air on his face as he crossed the courthouse lawn. The conversation with Ike had stirred something in him, and now the missing woman, Carla Warren, was at the forefront of his mind. He couldn't shake the feeling that there was more to her disappearance than what met the eye.

Back at the office, Clifford sat down at his desk, glancing at the clock. He had a few hours before the day ended and decided to go through some old case files to see if there was any mention of the Warrens or anything that could give him a lead. As he sifted through the papers, his thoughts wandered back to the last time he'd seen Deputy Warren. It was odd that someone who had seemed so settled in the community had suddenly disappeared without much of a trace.

His phone buzzed on the desk, pulling him out of his thoughts. It was Sheila.

"Clifford, I found something," she said. "There was a property sale up on Little Mountain Road about two and a half years ago. The buyer was indeed a Botetourt County Deputy named Warren. The place is pretty isolated—one of those old farmhouses that's been sitting empty for years before he bought it."

"Thanks, Sheila. That's just what I needed. Do you have the exact address?"

She gave him the details, and Clifford jotted them down on a notepad. "You're a lifesaver, Sheila. I'll swing by there this evening and see if I can find out anything."

After hanging up, Clifford leaned back in his chair, the wheels in his mind turning. There was something unsettling about the whole situation, and he knew he had to get to the bottom of it. He picked up his phone again and dialed Ike.

"Ike, I've got a lead on that missing woman, Carla Warren. It turns out her husband bought a place up on Little Mountain Road a couple of years back. I'm thinking we should take a drive up there tonight and see what we can find."

Ike agreed, and they planned to meet up in about an hour. Clifford hung up and prepared to head out. The day was cooling off, and the sun was beginning to dip low in the sky. He could feel that this was the start of something bigger—something that had been buried for too long.

As he locked up his office and stepped outside, Clifford felt a sense of determination. Tonight, they might just uncover the truth about Carla Warren.

Chapter Four

Clifford held his breath, hidden behind the doorway as he watched the tellers hurriedly stuff cash into shopping bags. He could hear the murmur of their anxious voices but kept his focus on the door, anticipating the arrival of the robber.

Moments later, the door creaked open, and Clifford saw the man from the reflection step into the room. He was dressed in a dark jacket and a cap, his face partially obscured by a mask. The man's eyes darted around, clearly on edge.

Clifford waited for the right moment, carefully considering his approach. He could see the man was tense, possibly panicking as he realised the tellers were emptying their drawers. Clifford had to act quickly but quietly to avoid any unnecessary risks.

As the robber turned to check on the progress of his haul, Clifford slipped out from his hiding spot and moved toward him. With a sudden burst of movement, he grabbed the robber from behind, applying a firm hold to restrain him. The man struggled briefly but was no match for Clifford's strength and training.

"Freeze! This is Sheriff Clifford Davidson!" Clifford said firmly, his voice commanding. "Put your hands where I can see them and don't make any sudden moves."

The robber froze, his eyes wide with shock. The tellers, who had been huddled behind counters, watched in a mixture of relief and fear. Clifford tightened his grip, ensuring the robber could not reach for any concealed weapons.

Just then, he heard footsteps approaching from the side office.

Clifford kept his eyes on the robber but signalled to one of the tellers to call for backup.

"Stay calm, everyone. I've got this under control," Clifford reassured them.

With the situation under control, Clifford took a moment to assess the scene. The tellers were visibly shaken but unharmed. He ensured the robber was securely restrained before calling in his deputies to handle the rest of the situation.

As he waited for backup to arrive, Clifford kept a close watch on the robber, reflecting on the narrowness of the escape from what could have been a disastrous situation. His instincts had been right to check on the bank, and he was relieved that he had intervened before things could escalate further.

He could hear bags shuffling and a voice saying, "Now get down on the floor and don't move." The person was coming toward the room where he was hiding, and as he came through the door, Clifford surprised him with his revolver pointed at the side of his head. To his shock, the man he had seen in the mirror was not the robber; he had a woman in front of him holding the bags full of money.

"Set the bags down and put your hands behind your back," Clifford told her. She complied, and he then made her sit down in the chair. He called for a deputy to come to the bank along with a State Policeman. The FBI would also be called in if necessary, but since this was a State Bank, Clifford didn't think the FBI would need to be involved.

Ike and James came running across the street and flung open the front door of the bank with their guns drawn. "Just cool it, boys; I have it under control here," Clifford said. "Take this woman over and put her in our holding cell. The State Police will be here shortly."

They escorted her across the street to the office and placed her in the holding cell.

The bank was locked down until the State Troopers arrived and did their investigation. The customers could still use the outside walk-up window to do their business until the bank could reopen. Tammy told Clifford that the woman had come in and seemed okay until she pointed the gun at her face. The assistant manager had walked into the lobby about that time, and she had put her gun in his ribs and told everyone to empty their cash drawers into the bags. "You came across the street about that time and saved the day. Had you not, we would have been missing a lot of money."

"I guess you are right," Clifford said. "But I was just doing my job and had a stroke of good luck to come in here at the right time."

The State Police arrived and Clifford informed them of what had just taken place. They started their investigation by taking the tellers' statements. "Should the FBI be called in on this situation?" Clifford asked the State Police officer.

"Yes, the bank is insured by the Federal Government, so they need to be involved," the officer replied. "We called them as soon as your office let us know. They should be here any minute."

John Jacobs from the FBI arrived shortly thereafter. Clifford briefed him on what had happened and then excused himself, heading back to his office. The State Police and FBI would come to his office as soon as they finished at the bank.

Clifford waited for another hour until the other officers finished at the bank and came to his office. "We have the woman in our holding cell. Do you want to question her here, or will you take her into your custody?"

"We'll take her to the FBI headquarters and take her statement there," Clifford replied. He led them to the holding cell, where they changed out the handcuffs, escorted the woman to the FBI car, and left. John told Clifford he would email him a copy of the transcript of her statement. Clifford was relieved not to have to deal with it himself, as he had enough on his plate right now. He gave Janet a quick call and told her what had happened.

"Clifford! You did what? Are you trying to make me a pregnant widow?"

"Just calm down, honey. I have to do my job. Your being pregnant does not change that."

"I know, but when you told me, I could imagine you lying on the bank floor in a pool of blood."

"I'm okay, honey. I'm all right, and I'm always careful. Besides, you're not the only one in the family who knows how to handle a weapon!"

He finished the conversation and told her he would be home around four o'clock. No sooner had he hung up the phone than it rang again.

"Clifford Davidson here."

"Hey, this is Sheila. I looked up the papers on the Warren name. He did not buy; he only rented the old Wallace farm for about six months."

"Thanks, Sheila. You've helped me a lot with another possible case."

Clifford went to Ike's office and sat down. Ike was just finishing up a call, so Clifford had to wait his turn. When Ike hung up the phone, he looked at Clifford. "What can I do for you, Mr. Sheriff, sir?"

Clifford smiled at Ike; this was his sense of humour at work. "I want to know if you remember if the Botetourt deputy told us he had rented up on Meadow Creek or if he had bought it."

"It's been a long time, but I believe he told us he had bought the place."

"That's what I remember also. Thanks." With that, Clifford left Ike's office and went back to his own.

He dealt with the paperwork on his desk, and before he knew it, several hours had passed. Picking up his phone, he dialled John Jacobs's number. He wanted to discuss his concerns about the Botetourt County deputy and the missing woman poster, which had the same last name.

John answered the phone after it had rung a few times and sounded out of breath. "This is Clifford. We received a poster on a missing woman by the name of Warren, who has been missing for two years."

"Yes, I remember the poster. What do you know about this woman?"

"I never met her, but two years ago, I talked with a Botetourt County deputy who told me he had just bought a place in Craig County. His name is also Warren. It seems a little weird to me, you know me and my gut feelings."

"Yes, Clifford, I know all about your gut feelings, and most of the time you're correct. I'll give Botetourt County a call and inquire about their deputy and let you know what I find out."

John hung up the phone, and Clifford finished the other small items awaiting his attention before checking out and heading home.

He could smell country-style steak frying on the stove when he came through the front door. "Hey, woman, where are you?" he called out. He did not get a reply, so he went across the hall and into the bedroom. Janet came out of the bathroom as he entered the bedroom.

"Evening, wife."

"Evening, husband," she replied, walking up to him and giving him a hug and a kiss. "How was your day after you talked with me?"

"Oh, so-so. Just the normal stuff after the bank robbery."

"I talked with my parents in Florida after we spoke. They are doing fine and enjoying the warm weather. They're looking forward to us coming down. I told them we were planning on a short visit next month, and they're fine with it."

"It's okay with them. I could tell by their voice after I told them about our visit. I did tell you that the Corp of Engineers is starting Monday on the Johns Creek Dam project?"

"No, you didn't. Which dam are they working on?"

"If I was told correctly, it will be the big one that was built first. They'll be bringing the equipment in this Monday to start pumping the water level down. The Corp can only put so much water in

Johns Creek at a time, or it could cause flooding."

By the time they finished discussing the project, the steak was done, and Janet was ready to put it all on the table. Clifford was hungry and ready to eat. Janet hadn't felt well that day and didn't want to eat much. She just picked at her food while he devoured his. Noticing her lack of appetite, Clifford asked, "Honey, what's going on with you and the food this evening?"

"I just feel bloated and don't want much tonight. It's a pregnancy thing, I'm sure."

He didn't like her answer but kept his thoughts to himself. If nothing else, he had learned to keep his remarks to himself unless she asked for them. Deep down, he didn't want to go to Florida next month but would, because he had promised her. Things were not going well at the office, and he would have preferred not to be out of the office any time soon.

They had a pleasant conversation at dinner and retired to the den for a little TV watching after he had helped her clean up from their supper. He could tell that she still did not feel all that good, so he left her alone when they got into the bed. He gave her a gentle hug and a light kiss on the lips and turned over to settle down for a long night of sleep.

Chapter Five

He was awakened by the sound of the alarm going off and was waiting for her to get up like she normally did. A few minutes had passed, and he could feel that she hadn't gotten out of bed. He turned over to her and laid his hand on her shoulder to see what the problem was. She did not move at his touch, and he got out of bed and went around to her side. He could see her breathing, but she would not respond to his touch or voice. He screamed to himself, "Oh God, no," and picked up the phone to call 911. The ambulance arrived in about fifteen minutes, but to Clifford, it seemed like an hour. He met them at the front door and took them to the bedroom.

"Clifford, go into the living room and sit down. You'll only be in the way. Let us do our jobs," the EMTs instructed. He agreed and went into the living room, starting to pray that she would be okay.

The EMTs checked her vitals and found that she was in a diabetic shock coma. They administered medication to bring her sugar level up but took her to Roanoke Hospital immediately. Her vital signs were starting to come back to normal, but she had not come out of the coma. She was starting to move her body around in the bed. They placed her in the ambulance and took off at high speed. Clifford followed in his cruiser, with every light on the car blinking. He stayed behind them while driving into the city, not wanting to get so excited that he would outpace the ambulance. Once in the city, he moved in front of them to stop traffic with his lights and siren, allowing both vehicles to keep moving and not stop for red lights.

By the time they arrived at Lewis Gale Hospital, Janet had

regained consciousness and was talking with the EMTs. They took her to the ER, and the doctors began their examination immediately. Cliff was right beside her and informed them that she was starting her third month of pregnancy. The doctors quickly began checking her abdomen for the baby's heartbeat. The doctor smiled at Clifford and told him, "Daddy, your baby's heartbeat is good and strong. It appears that this spell with your wife has not caused the baby any harm." Clifford thanked him and wiped away the tears forming in his eyes. If it meant losing Janet, he would rather not risk having children. He hoped the doctor was correct and that their child would be born normal. Janet, who had heard the doctor's reassuring words, felt relieved and had been about to cry. Cliff bent over and kissed her.

"Honey, I will be out in the waiting room. I need to get out of the way and let the doctors do the tests they feel necessary. I will be right through those doors over there. If you need me, send one of these nurses to get me. If they won't come, just scream my name loudly, and I will hear you."

He went into the waiting room, took his seat, and began to think if Janet had ever mentioned having any sugar problems. "I don't think she did. This must be something new, brought on by her pregnancy. Should I call her parents? No, not until she is back to normal and can talk with them herself." These thoughts and many more were running through his mind while he played the waiting game. The pediatrician came out of the ER and walked over to Clifford.

"She is fine now, and there is no reason why she can't go home. I know this is serious when it happens, but during a woman's pregnancy, her sugar level can go haywire. I believe if this happens again, she will now be able to recognize it. I'm sending a glucose monitor home with her and have instructed her to check her levels every morning and just before bedtime. We have checked her sugar levels, and they have returned to normal. I hope this is just a one-time thing. Her body is simply reacting to the hormonal change. The main thing is to monitor her sugar levels to prevent this from happening again. I will release her and bring her out to you. Go pull your vehicle up to the entrance door to pick her up."

Clifford did as instructed, and by the time he pulled up to the entrance, Janet was in a wheelchair with a nurse standing beside her. He got out, opened her side door, and helped her from the chair into the car seat. Once in the car, he kissed her and then began to drive home.

"Janet, I don't know what I would have done if they hadn't brought you back around to me. I'm glad our baby is okay, but I don't want to lose you because of the baby."

"No problem, Cliff. I feel fine, and I know to watch how I feel from now on. I've never had problems with my sugar levels before, and this is new to me. Once I deliver the baby, the doctor says my sugar levels should return to normal."

They arrived home to find a box on the front porch. Cliff helped Janet into the house, went back to the porch, and retrieved the box. The return address was from her parents in Florida.

Janet opened the box and found the baby gown she had been baptized in, along with a note from her mother: "I found this in one of our suitcases. It must have been stored in the case and we didn't notice when we filled it with our clothes. Hold on to it; you may need it sometime in the future."

Cliff looked at her and asked, "Do you think they know you're pregnant?"

"No Cliff, I don't think so. This is just a good omen that we're going to have a normal child in about seven months."

Janet seemed to be fine, so he went to work the next day.

"Hey Julie, how are things today?"

"They are fine here, but how about Janet? We heard what happened yesterday, but not what the outcome was."

"Her sugar went way high and she went into a coma, but the EMTs and the doctor in the ER stabilized her. The doctor said it was due to her body reacting to her pregnancy. He sent a glucose monitor home with her to keep track of her levels. She should now be able to recognize what is happening. He wants her to check her sugar morning and night and keep track of the readings. I can tell you right now that I was more nervous about her and this than I was about putting my gun to the bank robber's head the other day."

"Oh, by the way, John Jacobs called and gave us some information concerning the woman who attempted to rob Farmers and Merchants Bank. She is from Bluefield, W.V., and her name is Janice Holcomb. She hasn't revealed why she tried to commit the crime. The only thing she would say was her name and where she was from."

"Thanks, Julie. It's their case now; they can deal with it. I'm going to run up Johns Creek to see what's going on at the dam today. The Corps of Engineers is scheduled to start setting up their equipment."

Chapter Six

Clifford jumped into his cruiser and headed towards the watershed ponds up in Johns Creek Valley. It would take him around forty-five minutes to get to the ponds due to the narrow and winding road he had to navigate.

As he turned onto Johns Creek Road, he slowed his cruiser down to forty miles per hour. The road was so narrow and curvy that this was the maximum speed anyone should travel at. It wasn't quite as bad as the road across the mountain from Sinking Creek to Johns Creek, but it was a close second.

It took him thirty minutes to reach the intersection of Lower Johns Creek and Upper Johns Creek. The ponds were about ten miles down Lower Johns Creek Road.

Once past the one-room store where he and Janet had stopped the other day, the road turned to gravel, and he had another five miles to go to reach the ponds. He finally saw the dirt road leading up to the first and larger pond. He slowed his vehicle and carefully pulled onto the dirt road. Fresh tire tracks suggested that the Corps of Engineers must already be here.

He slowly drove up the bumpy, rutted road, taking almost ten minutes to reach the ponds. As he rounded the last curve, he had to brake hard and stop. In front of him was a soldier in a fatigued uniform, with a rifle pointed at him and his car.

The soldier immediately lowered the rifle, stepped over to the driver's window, and apologised to Clifford, stating he hadn't realised it was a police cruiser until it had finished coming around the curve.

"Sir, what may I do for you? This road and pond are secured property while the Corps is doing their job here."

"I understand. I spoke with Captain Jones the other day on the phone, and he advised me there would be armed guards while the Corps worked here. I'd like to go up to the pond if Captain Jones is there."

"Let me call him and check to make sure it's alright to let you pass through."

"Sure thing. I'll wait right here until you get the okay."

The soldier called Captain Jones and, after hanging up, motioned for Clifford to proceed. Clifford thanked him and drove past. The road was longer than Clifford remembered, but he finally reached the ponds he and Janet had walked around. He saw Captain Jones standing near one of the ponds, talking with a soldier who appeared to be inspecting a large water pump near the pond. Clifford noticed all kinds of piping being unrolled, indicating that they planned to pump the water out of the pond and across the field to Johns Creek.

He parked close to the pond, got out of his cruiser, and walked over to where the captain was standing.

"Morning, Captain Jones. I'm Clifford Davidson, Sheriff of Craig County. We spoke on the phone the other day. I was informed the Corps was moving in equipment, so I thought I should introduce myself. If there's anything our office can assist with, please call me."

"Thank you, Sheriff. I appreciate you coming up, but I hope we have everything under control and won't need your assistance.

However, I do need to ask you about something. Did you get a permit or written permission to cross that field? It is owned by someone else, not the pond owner. I'd advise you to get the paperwork before you start across the field, as I see no-trespassing signs all around it."

Captain Jones's face turned slightly flushed. "No, I hadn't considered crossing that field, but I will hold off until we acquire the necessary paperwork. I know we're Federal, but we might need a permit to dump pond water into the creek. I'd assume we have the authority, but I'll double-check with my boss. I haven't been in charge of this unit long, so I'd prefer to be safe and check with someone more experienced."

"Alright, well, I need to get back to my office. Good luck with the project."

Clifford left and slowly drove down the rugged dirt road until he reached the main road. He continued down the main road until he reached the little country store, where he pulled into the gravel driveway.

"Morning, Mary," he greeted as he walked in the store.

"Morning, Mr. Sheriff," she replied with a laugh. "I can't remember your given name."

"It's Clifford Davidson, but 'Sheriff' or 'Clifford' works too."

"Well, Sheriff, what brings you up this far in the county today?"

"I went up to the pond to check in with the captain in charge of the project. His name is Captain Jones, in case he comes into the store. He seems very nice. Since you're the only store close to them, I'd expect you'll see them come in for food while they're here."

"I saw a couple of trucks the other day and heard they were checking out the ponds. Yes, they're going to have to drain the first and largest one due to some structural problems with the earthen mound."

Clifford got a coke, paid for it, and sat down to chat with Mary for a while. He was still curious about why she moved away from her two sons to be close to just one.

He chatted for about ten minutes while drinking his coke but didn't get any insight from Mary about her move to Virginia. He decided to take the curvy mountain road to Sinking Creek and then to town on Route 42. He started up the curvy mountain road, slowing to twenty mph. The curves were blind, and he was on the side where, if he got hit by another car, he'd likely be pushed over the edge and fall a considerable distance unless a tree stopped his car. He didn't understand why the state didn't have guardrails on this side.

Just as he thought about the guardrail, he was starting into one of the sharp curves when a large F-150 appeared, taking up the entire road with no place for him to go. He slammed on his brakes, and the truck turned sharply to the right but still hit Clifford's back fender, causing his cruiser to spin around and end up with its back end over the embankment.

Clifford's life flashed before him as he tried to get his bearings. He could tell his car was in a precarious position and hoped he could get out before it went over the mountainside. He gently opened his door, expecting the car to topple, but it didn't. He jumped out as quickly as possible, and just as he cleared the car, it went over the side of the mountain. The cruiser fell almost a hundred feet before hitting a huge rock and bursting into flames.

Clifford felt a bit shaky but managed to calm himself. The thought of what could have happened to him and his family was overwhelming. He looked back at the pickup, which had ended up in the ditch after hitting his cruiser. He walked over to the truck, opened the driver's door, and was shocked to find a young boy, around ten years old, crunched down on the passenger side floorboard. The boy was shaking violently, clearly in shock. Clifford climbed into the truck, tried to comfort the boy, and pulled him out. Noticing an adult jacket in the truck, he put it on the boy and placed him back in the truck after securing it and turning off the engine, which had been running the entire time.

He called 911 and requested an ambulance, a state trooper, and a deputy to their location. He was sure the boy wasn't hurt, but shock could be serious in an accident. Clifford continued to talk to the boy, who began to regain some coherence. The boy spoke in a language Clifford didn't understand, which turned out to be Spanish when the EMTs arrived and spoke with him. The EMTs confirmed that the boy was speaking Spanish and said he appeared fine but needed to be checked out at the hospital.

"He's underage, and the truck tags are from North Carolina. I'd guess he's Mexican, and his parents are here working on a green card. If there are Spanish-speaking people in this county, they haven't been here long. This county is small, and news travels fast when someone new arrives."

"I'll call the hospital and advise them that a Spanish-speaking minor is being brought in and that they'll need to take charge of him until his parents arrive. That sounds like a good plan," the EMT replied.

When the rescue squad left with the boy, Clifford heard him

talking with the EMT and seemed to understand what was happening. The state trooper spoke with the boy through the EMT and learned that he was heading to his grandmother's, whom he had never met, but had been told lived over this mountain road. He and his father had argued, and he had taken the truck to find his grandmother. The only name he knew was her last name: Mann. This name struck a chord with Clifford.

The forestry pumper truck arrived and began putting out the fire caused by the cruiser's explosion. The trooper called for a larger wrecker to pull the cruiser up from the rock that had stopped its fall. Once the cruiser was brought up and loaded onto the wrecker, the trooper and wrecker left the scene, leaving only Ike, the new owner of the Huffman store, with Clifford.

"Ike, the boy said his grandmother's last name was Mann. Mary Mann owns the little store. I feel fine, but I think we should go back down to the store and talk with her."

They got into Ike's car and headed back down the mountain to the little store.

The two of them went into the little store and found Mary Mann sitting behind the counter.

"Hi guys, what can I do for you today?" she asked.

"We have a few questions to ask you concerning a truck accident we just came from on the mountain," Clifford replied. "I was run off the road, and my car went over the side of the mountain. The driver was a young boy who only spoke Spanish. He told us he was trying to get to his grandmother's store after arguing with his father."

Mary's face turned ashen. "Is the boy okay?" she asked.

"Yes, he seems to be, but the Rescue Squad has taken him to Lewis-Gale Hospital to be checked out. Do you know this child or anything about him?"

"I've never met him, but he is my daughter's son, whom she had with her boyfriend from Mexico. I wasn't happy when she had the boy and wasn't married to his father, so I wasn't included in his life. I don't know where they might be living right now, but if the boy was driving the vehicle, they must be near here."

"Is the boy hurt?" she asked.

"No, Mary. They took him to Lewis-Gale just as a precaution. If your daughter calls you, please tell her to contact my office. Will you be going to the hospital to check on him?"

"I don't know if they will let me see him if I can't prove I'm his grandmother, but I'll try. If you would like, I can go with you to vouch for you and your identification."

"Would you? I would appreciate it. Plus, I'm not sure how my grandson is going to react to me. I don't even know what my daughter named the child. I think his name is Hector, but I'm not sure."

"If you want, you can follow us back to town, and we'll go to the hospital in one of the county cars."

"Yes, that sounds good to me. Let me put a closed sign on the door and lock up the place. I will come to your office as soon as I take care of things here."

Ike and Clifford went on to the office. It was about two o'clock when they arrived.

"Thanks, Ike, for coming to retrieve me from the accident scene. I think it's time you went home; if I'm not mistaken, you came in early today. I will wait for Mrs. Mann and go over to Lewis-Gale with her."

"Okay, Clifford. See you in a day or two. I'm sure I'm off tomorrow, so be careful on your way to Salem."

Clifford picked up the phone and called Janet to tell her what had happened and to let her know he would be late coming home.

"Afternoon, wife. What are you doing?"

"I'm just relaxing out on the deck. What do I owe this call to?"

"Well, it's like this: I was in a wreck on Johns Creek Mountain Road, and now I'm taking Mrs. Mann, the owner of the little store we stopped at the other day, to Lewis-Gale to check on her grandson. He's a juvenile, and he was driving the truck that hit me. I'm fine, so don't get excited. I'll fill you in on all the details when I get home, but it will probably be around eight before I get back from Salem. Don't hold supper up for me."

"I'll put yours in the oven and keep it warm for you."

Clifford hung up the phone just as Mary Mann walked in the door.

"Are you ready?" she inquired.

"Yes, ma'am," he replied.

They went out and got in the extra cruiser that was kept in case of a breakdown of one of the others and started to Salem, Virginia, where the hospital was located.

Mary started talking to Clifford as they drove down Route 311, and

Clifford listened. He had found that listening often yielded more information than talking. Mary eventually shared that the real reason she had moved to Craig was to be closer to her grandson. She knew she was in the wrong concerning the split with her daughter and was trying to correct it. She also had a son in the area who had spoken with his sister but had never met his nephew or her partner. "I guess my son told my daughter where I was, so maybe this accident will help us reconnect."

They were turning into the hospital parking lot when a black Ford went in before them and pulled into a parking spot. Clifford parked next to the Ford. As Mary and Clifford were getting out of the cruiser, the man and woman from the truck were opening their doors.

Mary suddenly spoke to the woman and called her by name. "Clifford, this is my daughter, Jamey. This is Sheriff Davidson; he brought me over here to check on your son. He was driving the truck that Hector hit on the mountain above my store."

"I'm so sorry, Sheriff. I don't know what my son was thinking when he took the truck and thought he could get to his grandmother in it. My son does speak English, and the hospital workers finally got him to tell them our phone number so they could call us."

The man with her remained silent, his expression blank. Jamey spoke to him in Spanish, so Clifford assumed he didn't speak much English.

Clifford told Jamey that she and her partner needed to come to Craig to his office to fill out the necessary paperwork noting their insurance carrier. Their insurance would have to replace the county car that Hector had hit and destroyed. They agreed to come to Craig the next day and take care of everything. They also said they would arrange for Mary to get back to New Castle.

Clifford thanked them, got in his car, and called Janet to let her know he was coming back home and would be there for supper.

"Okay, Cliff, I will put everything on hold for thirty minutes and then start. It should be ready to go on the table about the time you get here."

"Okay, my sweet, I will see you in about forty-five minutes."

Chapter Seven

He walked in the front door, and Janet greeted him with a hug and a kiss. She knew he had had a rough day. "I'll have dinner on the table in about twenty minutes. Go on in and take a shower. I'll hold dinner for a few minutes longer until you come back to the kitchen."

"Sounds like a plan to me. I'll hurry up with my shower." He started taking off his clothes as he walked toward the bedroom, and by the time he was in the bathroom, he was completely naked. He had decided he must be a nudist at heart because he was most comfortable without clothing. The hot water felt really good, but he cut the shower short so he wouldn't keep her waiting.

He put on some gym shorts and a T-shirt and went back to the kitchen. Walking in, he could see Janet's side view. She had already started to show; the baby looked like a small watermelon in her stomach. She had told him the other day she felt it move inside her, and he had put his ear to her abdomen and thought he could hear a heartbeat. In a couple of weeks, they would be going down to Florida to visit her parents. He only hoped she felt good and that the trip wouldn't cause her any problems.

"Okay, woman, that food had better be on the table because I'm here and hungry."

"Be careful, bud, how you bark, or I may just dump it in the garbage can."

He grabbed her and kissed the back of her neck before sitting down at the table. The two weeks had flown by, and now they were pulling out of their driveway, heading south to Florida. He had packed the F-150 the night before, and the only thing to add this morning was Janet and himself. They lived up the mountain and off Route 42, and had decided to take Route 42 for thirty miles and then catch I-81 south. From there, they had three turn-offs until they reached the exit to Port St. Lucie, Florida. Once they got that far, it would take another half-hour to wind over to Hutchinson Island. In all, it should take them around fifteen hours, including stops for food and restrooms. They planned to get to Savannah, Georgia, by evening and find a room for the night.

He could see Route 460 ahead, where they would take a left and head into Christiansburg, then onto I-81 South. The half-hour drive down the deer-infested Route 42 had been uneventful—sometimes you have to dodge deer on this road. This four-lane road would lead them around Blacksburg and Christiansburg, where they would exit onto the interstate. Route 460 is a major route from Virginia to Bluefield, West Virginia, and is highly traveled.

They had covered twelve miles and were about to exit onto I-81 and start their journey on the East Coast interstate system. The next two hours would be on I-81, one of the busiest interstates for tractor-trailer rigs, running north and south on the East Coast from Tennessee to Pennsylvania. "I'm glad we only have about two hours on this road, then we'll exit onto I-77 south into North Carolina, I-26 in South Carolina, I-95 outside of Charleston, SC, and then on to Georgia and finally into Florida."

They made good time and were approaching Charlotte, North Carolina. He was glad they would be passing through this city before the lunch hour. Traffic can be awful here during busy times when people are heading to or from work or going to lunch.

They made it through Charlotte, even with the traffic being bumper-to-bumper, but it moved steadily. His speedometer registered sixty-five most of the way around the city, and he had to speed in the slower lane of traffic. The speed limit was posted at 55 mph, but he had to exceed it to avoid being run over. He had counted five police cars passing him, which were likely traveling at least seventy-five mph without any emergency lights flashing. "Oh well, I guess I need to learn to break the law and drive too fast on this traffic-filled highway."

He set the cruise control to seventy-eight mph once he was out of the city and cruising on the open road. Even then, he stayed in the right lane to avoid holding up the faster traffic in the left lane. The traffic had thinned out now that they were out of the city and were cruising on the open road. He was lucky; the new F-150 they had bought had light-up mirrors when a car was beside them, making passing safer. The truck also had a new type of cruise control that kept the vehicle in its lane unless directed otherwise, and it would even brake automatically if you approached a slower vehicle. You had to watch that feature, though, as it could slow you down below the speed limit without you realizing it.

They stopped just inside South Carolina for a light lunch before tackling a long stretch of rural driving. They stopped at Wendy's to avoid spending too much time eating and to have a light meal. They were back on I-77 and would travel another hundred miles before taking a left-hand exit onto I-26. This would take them fifty miles to the west of Charleston, SC, where they would pick up I-95 for the last leg of their journey. It was two-thirty now, and he estimated they would arrive in the Savannah area around six o'clock. It had been a long day, but Janet seemed to be doing well with the car motion.

"We're finally on I-95 just outside of Charleston, SC, and the traffic's moving along at seventy-eight mph. Janet is asleep, and I hope she can stay that way because this trip will be easier for her if she can nap through most of it."

Clifford noticed bright red brake lights ahead, and the traffic was slowing. "Now what?" he thought. The line of traffic in front of him came to a halt; he could see at least a mile of tail lights burning bright red. Janet woke and sat up in her seat. "What's happening, Cliff?" she asked.

"I don't know yet. All the traffic in both lanes has come to a standstill. It's probably an accident, which means we might be sitting here for a while."

"I hope not. I need to pee."

"Well, of course, you do, and we're nowhere near a bathroom. My dear, you'll have to hold it unless you want to squat beside the car. I guess we can open both passenger doors, and you can stand up and pee in a jug if we can find one. No one will be able to see you; the doors will block the view."

"Oh, Cliff, I just couldn't do that, at least not yet," she replied.

They both started laughing, and just then, the traffic began to move at a slow pace before speeding up to the limit. They hadn't gone far when they came to an exit with a Hardee's, and Clifford pulled into it. Janet nearly ran into the fast-food place and to the bathroom. Clifford used the men's room and got a cup of coffee to go. He knew she had cold drinks in their cooler, so she didn't need to buy one. It took her a little longer in the ladies' room than it had taken him in the men's room.

She jumped back into the truck. "Boy, do I feel better, bud. Thanks for stopping. How much farther to Savannah?"

"According to the GPS, we have about three more hours to get to Savannah, where we will stop for the night. We should arrive around 7 PM, which will be good. We can find a room off the interstate and then get some supper. I'm beginning to get hungry, and by the time we get there, my stomach will be growling."

Traffic moved on, and they did not have any more sudden stops to contend with. Clifford saw an exit sign and then one advertising an Embassy Suites. "Augh, that will be just great. Is Embassy Suites okay with you, Janet?"

"Great, they have nice beds, and I could use one after this day of traveling."

He took the exit and drove into the hotel parking lot. "Just wait here until I find out for sure that we can get a room." He went into the lobby, and after a while, he returned.

"We're in luck," he said, pulling the car into a parking spot close to the entry doors. They had packed one small bag with everything they would need for the night. "I see a Longhorn Steakhouse sign. Is that okay with you?"

"Lead on, oh great leader," she replied.

They went to their room, freshened up, and then went to the restaurant. The next morning, they arose at seven, checked out of the hotel, went over to Hardee's for a sausage biscuit breakfast, and then hit the road. There were still about eight hours to go to get to her parents' place. It would take them another three hours to reach the Florida state line and then another four to drive to Port

St. Lucie. Traffic seemed light as he pulled back onto I-95 and accelerated his speed to sixty-five. The speed limit would change to seventy in another ten miles, once they got out of Savannah proper.

Suddenly, the vehicles in front of Clifford and Janet started moving erratically, some to the left shoulder and some to the right pull-off lane. Clifford saw what was happening just in time to swerve to the right shoulder lane. There were four cars piled together in the middle of the four-lane road. He was able to brake and slide his vehicle to the right side of the interstate, avoiding all the debris. He kept going on the side of the road to get out of the way of the vehicles coming up behind him and could not stop. Once he had gotten ahead of the mess, he pulled into the grassy side of the road and told Janet to stay in the truck while he went back to help anyone who had been hurt. He saw at least ten people standing way over on the grass, where no one would come plowing through and hit them. He ran up to them and asked if there were people still in the wrecked vehicles. Their answer was no. He could see red lights and hear sirens, so he left the unhurt people and went back to his truck. Janet was upset but thankful that no one had been hurt.

He pulled back onto the interstate and continued down the highway. It wouldn't be too long before they crossed the border into Florida. They were approaching the outskirts of Jacksonville, FL, and he had to decide which direction to take. There were three choices: go straight through on I-95, take the east side of I-495, or the west side of I-495. All three ended up on the south side of Jacksonville and continued I-95 south. The I-495 makes a big circle around the city of Jacksonville, FL. He decided to go through on I-95 since they were not in prime time for traffic and he thought it would be faster. It took them twenty minutes to make it through and continue down I-95 to Daytona Beach, then Cocoa Beach, Cape Canaveral, Melbourne, Vero Beach, and finally Port St. Lucie, where they would get off the interstate.

Now that they had come through Jacksonville, the traffic was starting to thin out, and driving was a little easier. They were expected to arrive on Hutchinson Island around five o'clock, and he would be glad to get out of the truck for a few days. They made their way down to Vero Beach, and the GPS indicated that they would turn off on Crosstown Parkway in eighteen minutes. It felt like he had just looked at the GPS and saw eighteen minutes, and now the exit was here. He took the off-ramp and turned onto Crosstown Parkway, which would lead him eight miles to Route One. It was a beautiful tree-lined, three-lane highway on each side.

They reached the intersection of Crosstown and Route One quickly. The next leg was to cross One, and Crosstown turned into Village Green Drive. They drove about two miles and then turned left onto Walton Road, following it until they reached the three-way stop intersection at the Intracoastal Waterway. He took a right and followed that highway until reaching the turnabout. Listening to the GPS, he went around the turnabout and over the huge bridge onto Hutchinson Island. Her parents had told them to go north on A1A once on the island until they saw a lot of condos. They would be looking for the one with the sign reading North Star Condo Estates. He followed the GPS commands, and when he pulled into the driveway, the GPS said, "You have reached your destination."

They found a parking space marked "Visitors" and pulled into it. They took one suitcase with them to the building entrance; they could come back for the rest of the luggage. "Your parents' condo is 565, which means it is on the fifth floor and is number 65." They took the elevator up to the fifth floor, and when the door opened, 565 was right in front of them. He pushed the doorbell and could hear it ringing.

Her mother opened the door, took one look at Janet, and let out a scream for Mr. Moore to come quickly. Mrs. Moore was hugging Janet when her father came into the hall. "Mother, let me hug her too." Mrs. Moore stepped away, and he saw that his little girl was in the way. He let out a war whoop that all the neighbors had to have heard. He gave Clifford a big grin and congratulated them both on almost being parents. "The coffee is on, Cliff, or can I just call you son?"

"Son is fine," Cliff answered.

They sat down at the table, and her mother poured them all a cup of coffee. "Now, honey, you said you were coming today, but you didn't tell us how long we can expect you to stay."

"Have we already outworn our welcome? We just got here," her dad said, shaking his finger at her but not saying a word.

"We can stay for two weeks unless something happens in New Castle that causes Cliff to have to go home."

"Sounds like a plan to us. We have the guest bedroom all ready, not that you are guests."

Her mother led her down the hallway and showed her the bedroom they would be using. Clifford excused himself to go get the rest of their luggage, and her father went with him. Mr. Moore took along a rolling dolly to carry everything so they wouldn't have to make any more trips to the truck. He didn't say much to Clifford on the elevator ride down to the truck, but Clifford could tell there was something on his father-in-law's mind.

They were back in just a few minutes with the rest of the luggage. "Well, Mom, I am ready for another cup of coffee if there is any left. We hit it pretty hard when we first arrived."

"Well, son, I will make some more if the well has run dry."

She got up and sure enough, had to put on another pot. The coffee was ready, and all four sat back down at the table for coffee and conversation.

"Janet, how is it going with your new house—or is that old new house? I do believe that could be considered an oxymoron."

They all laughed at her mother's English lesson. Her mom wanted to know how far along she was and how the pregnancy was going. Janet hesitated before telling her about her sugar problem at first but decided to be open about the issue she had experienced in the first month. Her mother understood and told her not to worry about it; other women she knew had the same reaction when they first became pregnant. Sometimes it takes a woman's body a little while to accept the changes it goes through when growing another person inside.

Her father wanted to know if they knew the sex of the child, and they told him they did not want to know. The doctor knew but they declined to find out; they wanted it to be a surprise.

"Honestly, Mom, sometimes I feel like I'm getting as big as an elephant."

"Well, darling daughter, maybe you will have one of each. You know, twins do run in my family."

"No, Dad, I did not know. Oh, crap, Cliff, what would we do with two babies at the same time?"

"Well, dear, I guess your parents would have to raise one of them."

"I'm glad you said that, son. Mom and I have a question to ask you. What would you say to us about remodeling the barn and changing it into a summer apartment for us to come to? If we did that, then we could help out with the kids for a few months each year."

Cliff and Janet just looked at one another with their mouths half open. "Uh, um, well, Mom and Dad, I speak for both of us. That would be just great, and if you like, you can use some of John's life insurance money to do the remodeling with."

"That won't be necessary, but we do appreciate the offer. We'll get started on the plans. We will want one bedroom, an eat-in kitchen, a living room, and a bath. We will stay in Florida from November till June unless you need us more than those months. We can stay longer in Virginia if necessary. I think we can handle it ourselves if it is only one baby, but we know you want to be a part of your grandchild's life, so when they get a few years older, we will let you take them for a week or two if it turns out to be more than one child. We will just have to play all of this by ear."

"So, guys, we have plenty of sunlight left. Do you want to hit the beach for an hour and soak up some rays?"

"Yep, let's change our clothes, and the four of us will go down for some sun and relaxation."

The four of them took their chairs and headed down to the beach. It was only ten feet from the condo door to the sand. Clifford had put on a bathing suit just in case he wanted to go into the ocean.

"Man," Mr. Moore commented, "what a swimsuit!" He pointed at Clifford's striped trunks. They were red and white stripes running around his body, not up and down.

"Cliff, honey, where did you get those trunks? I haven't seen them before, or I would have burned them!"

"I'll have you know that I've had these since I was in high school. I wear the same size now as I did then, so how about them apples?"

Janet just shook her head and uttered, "Oh well," knowing when she had lost the argument. They enjoyed themselves for an hour and then went back to the condo to shower and change clothes. Cliff and Janet showered together but refrained from any loving in the shower.

"Well, guys, where do you want to go out to eat tonight?"

"Dad, I don't know the restaurants. You pick; anything is good with us."

"If you don't care, we can go over to the mainland to Conche Joes. They have everything and really good fresh seafood."

"Sounds great to me!" Cliff exclaimed. "I haven't had any good seafood since we were on our honeymoon at the Outer Banks, North Carolina."

Her mom chimed in, "I vote for Conche Joes. I love the thatch roof and being able to look out on the inlet waterway while eating."

"Okay," her dad replied, "the boss has spoken. Let's hit the road and go get our tummies full. I'm buying, so order the most expensive thing on the menu. I'm feeling generous today. I'm going to be a granddaddy, hurray!"

Both women had to use the restroom before they could head to the mainland. They jumped into the new Ford F-150. It had four doors, and all of them fit in it comfortably for the trip. There was a lot of traffic on the causeway bridge that connected the island to the mainland, but it only took them about twenty minutes to make the trip.

Chapter Eight

They arrived at the restaurant and were seated in the dining room built out over the water.

"This is great, Daddy, but the prices on the board are high," Janet said.

"Don't worry, daughter. This evening, the sky's the limit. Nothing will be too expensive for my pregnant daughter," her dad replied.

"Does that include me, Cliff?" asked Janet. "I did get her pregnant, so my meal should be just as good."

Mr. Moore just grinned at Clifford and didn't say a word. The food was delicious, and the view was terrific, so the four of them enjoyed their meals and the scenery.

"Mom, how are you and Dad adjusting to living in a condo in Florida?" Janet asked.

"Just fine now, but at first, I had some misgivings about being here. We missed you, of course, but there were the farm animals we had. People don't realise how attached you can get when you care for a farm animal every day—even chickens can become precious. I'm over that now, except for missing you, of course. Your dad and I have a nice little daily schedule. We get up at eight, I fix breakfast, then we go down to the exercise room for an hour, and then back to the condo for showers and a half-hour rest. By noon, we call your uncle, and most of the time, the four of us go out for a little lunch. After lunch, it's beach time for as long as we like, usually about an hour and a half. Then we play a few games of dice and have some liquid refreshments. Sometimes we get a wild hair and take off thrift store shopping or head down to West Palm Beach for some shopping. We have stores here, but nothing like West Palm Beach."

"Well, Mom, it sounds like you guys have settled in down here and are enjoying yourselves. You do know that you're welcome to come up any time for a week or two. Once you get the barn remodeled, of course, it will be yours for whenever or however long you want to stay. Once this grandchild is born, you might come up to Virginia and never come back to Florida."

"I'm sure we'll spend some time in Virginia, but we're used to the weather down here, and I don't think we'll want to give it up."

Their meal finished, Mrs. Moore wanted to visit the vegetable stand just around the corner, about a mile away, to see what fresh veggies they had. Their stay went this way for the two weeks: out to eat, thrift stores for the women, and shopping at Beall's for clothes. The guys played several rounds of golf, and then it was time for Janet and Cliff to return home.

They didn't want to travel on weekends, so they left on Monday to start their journey home. The trip went smoothly; they stopped at every rest area when changing states and, of course, for lunch. They got as far north as Charlotte, North Carolina, and stopped at a Cracker Barrel for supper. It was only six-thirty when they finished eating, and since it was only three hours away from home, they decided to finish the trip and not waste money on a hotel room. It turned out to be a mistake—during the last hour of the trip, Cliff fought to keep his eyes open. They rolled into their driveway around midnight and fell straight into bed. They had stayed up late the night before talking with her parents and had started their trip the next morning at eight o'clock. Her mother had insisted they eat breakfast with them before starting their trip, which meant they had to get up around six-thirty and hadn't gone to bed until one a.m. They didn't have to get up the next morning; Clifford had taken off Monday and Tuesday of that week. They both woke up around ten o'clock and turned to each other. They both knew what was going to happen; their lovemaking wasn't as frequent while visiting her parents.

Cliff reached over and pulled her close, caressing her back while kissing her and then moving his hot lips down her neck. It was nearly eleven-thirty before they showered and got dressed.

"Cliff, honey, do you know what I'd like to eat?" Janet asked.

"No, I can't say as I do, since I can't read your mind, and I'm sure glad of that fact. I'm game; what does my little wife want?"

"I'd like to drive into Roanoke to the Waffle House and get a huge waffle with strawberries, whipped cream, and syrup."

He just smiled and said, "Let's go, boss." With that, they got into the car and headed out to the Waffle House. It took them about forty-five minutes to get there, but Janet said it was worth the trip, as far as she was concerned.

"Your wish was my command," Cliff said in a husky tone.

"Since we're in the city, is there anything you need or want?" Janet asked.

"We need to go by Walmart to get some groceries if you expect me to cook at home. There's nothing in the cupboard for us to eat until we buy something, my dear."

He headed out of the Waffle House driveway and went directly to

Walmart. "We have arrived, my dear."

"It's about time," she replied in a mocking tone. "Now, get out of your car seat and get a buggy for me to fill up with your favourite food."

He did as he was told, knowing he needed to pull his weight in the grocery shopping. An hour later, and one hundred and fifty dollars spent, they started back to New Castle. He helped get everything into the kitchen and let her put it away, knowing that it was her kitchen and that she had specific places for everything. He had picked up the mail from the Post Office as they passed through town and was now sorting through it. He tossed the junk mail immediately and then looked at the one or two bills that had arrived. Nothing urgent had come, so he picked up the Mecum Car Auction book that had arrived and began thumbing through its pages. There were some beautiful vehicles, but none that a new daddy-to-be could afford.

Feeling bored, he called out to Janet and asked if she would like to go down to the barn to get an idea of what could be done to transform it into an in-law apartment for her parents. She came into the den, ready to go with him. He held the door open, and they started the short walk to the barn.

"You know, Janet, I think we should use some of the money you received from your brother's insurance to redo this and surprise your parents when they come up. We'd probably spend more and make it nicer than they would."

"I think you're right, and I'd love to do it for them. You know me and decorating."

"Then we agree. You can call a contractor and have them come over to see if the barn is sound enough to revamp."

"I'll call Everett Jackson when we get back to the house and set up a time for him to come, say in two weeks. That will give us time to draft a rough idea of what we want the place to look like."

"Sounds like a plan to me," she said as he finished his suggestion. She had an appointment with the baby doctor the next day, but she felt okay and told Cliff to go to work. She could make the appointment on her own. He felt she was right but knew that when she was later in the pregnancy, he would need to take her. He picked up the phone and called Mr. Jackson, setting up an appointment for the Monday after next. This should give them enough time to map out what they wanted done to the barn.

Chapter Nine

Clifford was dreading going back into the office after being away for two weeks. The office hadn't called him while he was away with anything needing his attention. Julie was on duty and buzzed him in the door when he walked up to the porch of the office.

"Morning, Julie. Nice to see you again. Hope the sugar is still under control," he commented as he walked past her on his way to his office.

Sitting down at his desk, he noticed a huge number of sticky notes in his work area. Looking at the first one, it read: *Call John Jacobs at the FBI office when you get back*. He picked up the phone and dialed the number on the note.

"Morning, this is Captain Jacobs. May I help you?"

"Morning, this is Sheriff Davidson in Craig County. I had a note to call you when I got back from vacation."

"Yes, Sheriff, I was just going to update you on Deputy Warren that we were looking into. So far, we haven't located him, and the Botetourt County office cannot find a record of him. It's like he never existed, except for the property rental in your county and the fact that you had lunch with him. There's something weird going on with this guy; we'll keep tracing him and trying to run down his whereabouts."

"Okay, I thank you very much for the update. Hopefully, you can come up with something. My gut tells me there's something going on with this guy."

The next five or six notes were concerned residents and complaints about noise and barking dogs, which he couldn't address since the county didn't have a noise ordinance. He saw that the deputy in charge had informed these people of the facts about the noise. He didn't like not being able to help these people, but his hands were tied.

One note stated that Captain Jones of the Corps of Engineers had called to tell him everything was going as planned and after further examination, they would determine if the other pond would also need to be drained and repaired. That wouldn't happen until they finished repairs on the current one. The second note simply said the second pond would also need repairs. He felt that the captain was a caring person and wanted everything done properly, and he appreciated being kept informed.

He dialed the number on the note, and in two rings a voice answered, "This is Captain Jones. May I help you?"

"Morning, Captain. This is Sheriff Davidson. I just wanted to thank you for your call to let us know things were going okay at the dam site."

"You're quite welcome, Sheriff. I assume you saw on the note that the other pond will need to be drained as well."

"Yes, Captain, I did see that. I guess it might be a good thing; that way, you guys will know both of them will be good for a couple more decades before another update might be necessary."

"I agree," the Captain replied. "There doesn't seem to be quite as much erosion on the berm of the second pond as the first, but we need to address the situation now and not later."

"Captain, how are things progressing on the pond you are currently working on?"

"It's almost dry now, and we are taking soil samples and examining its walls to see if there is any danger of the walls collapsing. Our opinion is that we need to completely dry the pond and then install a plastic liner designed for these dirt berms to prevent leakage from the side of the walls. It will not cost the landowner anything since we are responsible for maintaining watershed ponds."

"That's a good thing. Most of these people couldn't afford such an item. I'm sure they are expensive to install, not to mention the cost of the materials."

"You're correct. The cost is rather high. I'm glad the government has stepped up and accepted responsibility for these ponds they installed decades ago."

"Okay, I appreciate all the updates. Let me know if my office can assist you with anything."

So far, so good, he thought as he finished looking through the rest of the paperwork on his desk. He was lucky to have a good team that had taken care of all the daily items. Now, he was heading out on the street to talk with some of the people he hoped had put him in office for the second time. He had learned that if you wanted to know what people were thinking, you had to go face-to-face with them and listen. Over the past three years, he had learned many things about the county and its people just by being a good listener.

Clifford walked through the front entrance of the Farmers and Merchants Bank and saw Tammy at the first window. Strolling over to the window, he gave her a big smile and a "Good afternoon." She returned the smile and greeting, offering him a piece of candy from the bowl on her ledge.

"I believe I will," he said as he reached for a piece. "I hope everything is going well here today. At least, I hope there hasn't been a robbery asking for cash."

"Oh no," Tammy replied, "thank goodness that hasn't happened again. I hope I never see another one while I work here."

"That makes two of us, Tammy. Well, I need to move on. You guys have a good day."

He left the bank, crossed the street, and went into the front entrance of the courthouse. He waved to the Treasurer and Commissioner of Revenue as he walked through the hallway leading to the back entrance of his office. Things had been quiet today, and that was how he wanted it. He hoped the increased patrols around the county had made a difference in deterring lawbreakers. It had been a couple of years since any murders had occurred, and he hoped that would last longer. It was almost time to go home and be with his wife for a few hours. She was using the vacuum cleaner when he came through the front door and didn't hear him come in. He sat down until she finished and turned off the machine, then said, "Good evening, wife!"

She smiled and said, "Good evening, husband!" Then she sat in his lap and gave him a juicy kiss. "How was your day at the office?"

"Just fine, and everything was quiet. How about here? Did you have a good day?"

"Yes, I did. I slept late, did a load of laundry, and cleaned the bathrooms and kitchen. Took a break for some coffee and then started drawing up the plans for my parents' apartment in the barn.

I haven't gotten much done, but at least I've started. Maybe you can sit down with me tonight and we can come up with something together."

"That's an affirmative, my dear. We'll work on it after we get supper and have full tummies."

She had dinner ready, and all she had to do was set it on the table. They ate quickly, excited to start the project. They decided to just do it and, when her parents decided to proceed, they would tell them it was already done. The contractor had come a few days earlier and told them the building was structurally sound for a remodel, so now they needed to decide how they wanted it done. They wanted it done right and only with the best materials. Once the contractor replaced the foundation with something stronger, they could divide the space into rooms. They wanted all the living space on the ground floor, with poured concrete as the base for the remodeling. The first floor would have its own stud walls for good insulation, and the upstairs could be used for storage. They decided on two bedrooms—one for her parents and one for guests, such as an overnight grandchild—a large eat-in kitchen that opened to a great room, a big fireplace in the great room, and a sun porch off the kitchen. The contractor agreed that all these elements were doable and would start the work at the beginning of the next month, once he completed his current job. They shook hands, signed the contract, and gave him a check for fifty thousand dollars to begin the project. The contractor had done as promised and was now in his third month of building. The project was moving right along since the outside walls and roof were already in place. It took only a week to complete the foundation and concrete floor. He had already divided the rooms, put in the interior studding, and wired everything. Next week, he was to start drywalling the inside and hoped to have the project done within the next two months. Janet had enjoyed working with him and making daily decisions about the items the contractor brought up, ensuring there were no delays. Janet was slowing down some now; she was about to enter her ninth month and couldn't get around as fast as usual. She had already picked out all the furnishings for the new apartment and hoped to have it finished and furnished before she went into labor. The contractor thought he would be done in less than two weeks, and she hoped so; she wanted it ready for her parents to stay in when they arrived for the baby's birth.

"Hurray, the apartment is finished and it looks beautiful!" Janet exclaimed. They had received all the furniture the day before and placed it exactly where she had instructed. She took some of her mother's sheets and towels and set up the rooms, preparing everything for their arrival.

Clifford took the day off to accompany Janet to her doctor's appointment. The doctor examined her thoroughly and turned to both of them. "Well, guys, it's any day now. Janet has started to dilate, so it just depends on how fast the process takes."

The couple left the doctor's office on cloud nine. All these months of waiting were almost over. They went to Sassy's Restaurant to enjoy a nice steak. The owners had sold, but they were still there for a couple of months. They both wanted a ribeye, medium well, with a baked potato and salad with blue cheese dressing. Clifford had a glass of wine, but Janet settled for water with lemon.

As they were finishing their meal, Janet's cell phone rang. She glanced at the caller's name. "It's my mother. I need to take this call."

"Hello, Mom. We're fine, just finishing up a steak at Sassy's Restaurant. We had been to the doctor for my last checkup. Everything is fine except for one thing!"

"Oh dear, what's the problem, honey?" her mother asked.

"The problem is that I'm due any day, and I don't know if you and Dad can start up here by tomorrow. I've started dilating already, and the doctor said it would only be two or three more days if all goes as planned."

"Daughter, I'm hanging up the phone and we'll head out tonight. We should be there by tomorrow evening sometime. We'll spend the night somewhere; just cross your legs until we get there."

"Okay, Mom. You and Dad, be careful on your trip up."

The Moores packed their clothes and headed out immediately. They didn't want to miss the birth of their grandchild. They made it as far as the outskirts of Charlotte, North Carolina, before stopping for the night. Finding a good Holiday Inn Express off the exit and a nice mom-and-pop restaurant nearby, they settled down for the night.

Mr. Moore set the alarm on his phone for 6 a.m. They wanted to get an early start and reach Virginia as soon as possible. He checked the GPS, which showed four hours remaining on the trip. The Moores would be glad when they finally pulled into their old driveway.

Chapter Ten

Clifford heard the alarm go off and got up, heading to the kitchen to make coffee. Janet was now in her ninth month, and she was as big as a whale—of course, he wouldn't tell her that. They expected her parents to arrive sometime late in the evening, but he needed to go into work today because he would be taking quite a few days off very soon. Going back to the bedroom, he saw that Janet was still asleep. He took care of his morning routine quietly and then got dressed before heading back to the kitchen for his coffee. He was on his second cup when she waddled into the kitchen.

"Morning, sleepyhead," she said, giving him a look he didn't want to dwell on. She got herself a cup of coffee and sat down with him at the table. They both sipped their coffee, cuddling their hands around the cups.

"I tried not to wake you," Clifford said. "I was as quiet as I could be."

"Oh, you didn't wake me. I was lying there trying to get back to sleep, but it's hard for an elephant to get comfortable," she replied.

"I wouldn't know about that, but I'll take your word for it," Clifford said with a smile. "I need to get going into the office. If you need me, call me, even if you're not sure what's happening. It'll take me at least fifteen minutes to get back here, so don't wait until the last minute."

"I won't, Cliff. I'd just as soon not have this baby in your squad car on the way to the hospital."

"I'm going to work now. Give me a call if your parents arrive and

I haven't returned home."

"Okay, I will, honey. But I don't think they'll be here until late this evening. I might call Mom and see where they are and when they think they'll arrive. I can hardly wait for them to see their new apartment, too. Got to run now."

She didn't say anything else before he left, but she didn't feel all that great this morning. There was a lot of pressure down below, and she wasn't sure what it was about.

Clifford went into the office, sat down at his desk, and started sorting through the paperwork that always seemed to accumulate while he was gone. Sometimes he thought they saved it up for him so that he'd have a large pile to deal with and think he was doing a really good job.

The phone rang, and he put down the paper to pick up the phone.

"Sheriff Davidson, this is Captain Jones at the watershed pond. I just wanted to give you a call and let you know that we're almost finished with the first pond. By next week, we'll start pumping down the second one. We thought it would be the smaller of the two ponds, but it's much deeper and holds just as much water—it's just shorter in length than the one we're repairing now. If you'd like to come up and see what we've done, you're welcome to."

"Captain, I'd love to, but my wife is expecting any day now, and I need to stay close to the office for a while."

"I understand, Sheriff. I have four kids of my own. I know what's happening, but if you get a chance, come on up."

The phone rang again, and this time it was Janet. "Hey, honey, my parents just pulled into the driveway."

"Okay, I'll come home early. Nothing seems to be happening here today." He told Julie what was going on and headed home to greet the in-laws. When he pulled into the driveway, he noticed that the Moores had either bought a new vehicle or rented one just for the trip. A new Lincoln Corsair was parked in the driveway. He went inside, hugged them, grabbed a cup of coffee, and sat down at the table with them.

"How was your trip up? It seems like you must have made pretty good time to get here this early. That Lincoln must travel faster than the F-150 Ford. Did you trade the truck in?"

"Yes, we did. The truck was starting to get some miles on it, but it was still worth about thirty thousand dollars. We don't need a truck anymore, so we tried this little car out, and it seemed to suit us, so we bought it."

"Don't blame you one bit. Did you get a glimpse of the old barn as you drove in?"

"No, we were just so glad to be here before Janet went into labor that we didn't think about it."

Janet spoke up, "Mom and Dad, we have a surprise for you. We had the barn remodeled and furnished. All you have to do is live in it when you want to."

Their mouths dropped open, and they were speechless for a minute or two. "You did what?"

"We've already had your apartment built in the old barn, and it came out rather nice, even if I was responsible for doing it."

Her dad smiled at her and Cliff and gave them both a hug. "Thanks so much. I was dreading dealing with your mother once we started on the project. We'll write you a check for the cost; just tell us the amount."

"You most certainly will not. Your son paid for all the remodeling. We felt like he would want this for you two, so we don't want to hear another word."

Mrs. Moore teared up and said, "Thanks so much. You two will never know what this means to us."

Cliff spoke up, "And you two will never know how much we love you guys either. Now you have a summer home or an anytime home, which would be more our wish."

With that, the four of them went down to the barn to see the new apartment. Mr. and Mrs. Moore walked through the front door and couldn't believe what they saw.

"Oh, Janet, it's simply beautiful! You did all this yourself?"

"Yes, Mom. I picked everything out. I wouldn't let Cliff do anything. I know what kind of taste he has, just like Dad's, and I knew you and I wouldn't like what he would choose."

They chatted for another couple of hours, and then the Moores moved their clothes into the new apartment. Janet made it clear to them that the apartment was mainly for sleeping and that their baby services would be needed most of the day once she delivered. Her parents assured her they would be underfoot as long as she needed them to be.

She had prepared a good old country dinner: country-style steak cooked in the crock pot, with sides of mashed potatoes, green beans, coleslaw, and, of course, some scratch buttermilk biscuits.

By the time they had eaten, all four of them felt like little pigs. Her parents went down to their apartment, tired and ready for hot showers and an early night. Janet and Cliff watched a little TV before retiring around eleven o'clock. She still felt uncomfortable from the pressure the baby was causing her.

"Cliff, honey, I've experienced a lot of pressure today from the baby, but my water hasn't broken, so I don't think I'll be in labor tonight. But just in case, I thought I should warn you to be ready."

"Why are you just now telling me this? Shouldn't we call the doctor or even go to Salem to the hospital?"

"Calm down, Cliff. This is why I haven't told you until now—you always get so excited. We will have plenty of time once my water breaks to get to the hospital."

"We better, or you might end up having this baby by the side of the road under a tree."

They both just smiled at that. She turned onto her other side and fell asleep quickly, but Cliff was still edgy and lay there for another hour before he fell into a deep sleep.

Janet awoke and looked at the clock—it was only 1:30 a.m. She was thirsty, so she got up and started to the kitchen. She was halfway down the hall when her water ran down her legs and onto the floor. She turned around, went back to the bedroom, and woke Cliff up. He didn't know why she had awakened him, and all of a sudden, he realized what was happening. She had to gently smack him in the face to get his attention.

"One, call 911 for an ambulance. Two, call my mother's cellphone, not my dad's, and tell them to get up here ASAP."

He did exactly as she told him, though she did have to remind him of the address. He was so excited he couldn't think clearly. Her mother came running in the door and took over.

"Cliff, go boil water, now."

Cliff went to the kitchen and put a pot of water on. Mrs. Moore didn't need the water; she just wanted him out of the way. She grabbed some Clorox cleanup and paper towels and cleaned up the water from the floor after she had seen to her daughter's needs.

Her father arrived about five minutes after Mrs. Moore and wanted to know what he could do. His wife told him to go into the kitchen, calm Clifford down, and stay there unless she hollered for one of them. He didn't like what she said, but he knew when she used that tone of voice, he had better do as she said.

"Honey, when was the last contraction?"

"Mom, it was about two minutes ago, and I'm having another right now," she screamed as the contraction hit her.

"Try not to push; just relax if you can. I hope the ambulance gets here soon, but if your contractions are that close together, I doubt they will."

Mrs. Moore screamed at Cliff, "Bring in about four clean towels and start taking deep breaths. You're going to need them when we deliver this baby."

Mr. Moore went back to the kitchen, and Mrs. Moore told him to stay there and let the ambulance in when they arrived.

Clifford took the towels into the bedroom, and what he saw shook him. Janet was in bed with two pillows under her back and part of her buttocks to support her, and her mom was there waiting for the baby to come out.

"What can I do?" he asked.

"Just stand there in case I need to hand you the baby," Mrs. Moore replied.

Thank God, the EMTs arrived and quickly took over.

"Ma'am, you're going to deliver right here. Once we help you, we'll take you to Salem with your baby for your doctor to check the two of you out."

"I understand," she replied, just as a terrible pain hit her.

The EMT told her to push hard and hold it. Finally, the pain subsided, and he told her to relax. She hardly relaxed when another pain struck, and she screamed out, "Push!" The EMT told her to push again. Janet could hear the baby crying and saw the EMT cutting its cord and wiping it down with a clean washcloth.

The EMT started to hand the baby to Janet when another pain hit her, and she screamed again. The EMT handed the baby to the other person helping with the ambulance call.

"Janet, you're having a second baby. When I tell you, push really hard and keep pushing until I tell you to stop."

Just then, the pain hit again, and Janet did as she was told.

"You can stop pushing now, Janet," the EMT said. "Your first baby is a girl, but this baby is a boy."

Cliff was standing at the door, fainted, and fell to the floor. When he came around, he was being picked up off the floor.

"Yes, Daddy, there are two—a girl for her and a boy for you. Congratulations, Sheriff."

He went into the kitchen to tell the Moores that they were grandparents twice over. Janet and the babies were fine but were headed to the hospital in the ambulance to be checked out. The Moores stayed at home, and Clifford headed to the hospital. He caught up with the ambulance and followed them there. Once they were all inside, he filled out the paperwork and called the Moores to let them know everything was well. He planned to stay until the doctor checked out all three of them.

"Okay, Cliff, calm down now. Everything is over, and all you and Janet have to do is raise them to be good people."

"That could be the tricky part, the way things are in this world today," he replied.

The doctor shook his hand and left the room, leaving the new family together.

"Dear, we had decided on Daniel or Danielle, depending on which sex we had. I guess we get to use both names since we have one of each."

"You're right, honey. And boy, I'm happy your mom is here. I have a feeling we're going to need some assistance for a while."

"I agree," Janet replied, smiling from ear to ear. "By the way, thanks for giving me two children for the price of one."

With that, he bent over and gave her a hard kiss.

"Whoa, let's not start another right away," she said.

They had Daniel and Danielle in the room with their mother, so when her parents walked in, they got to hold their grandchildren. "We just had to come on to see our grandbabies up close and personal."

"We know, and it's okay with us. We are going to need some help since there are two of them. Meet Daniel and his twin, Danielle. Kids, meet your grandparents."

The babies smiled—or so the Moores told everyone. Babies don't smile when they are a few hours old; all they want is a warm spot, milk, and a dry diaper. Her parents did not stay long, and once they had gone, Cliff kissed Janet goodbye and headed home to get some shut-eye. His in-laws got home before him and went directly to their new apartment in the barn. They loved their new digs, especially the big patio off the kitchen at the rear of the barn. The view was wonderful; you could see rolling green hills for miles and then purple mountains behind them. They were accustomed to the sight, but they were always busy and did not take time to sit and enjoy the view. Now they could just relax and look at it as much as they wanted, at least until the phone rang and they were summoned to help with the children. They knew that they could be a big help for a few months until the new parents got the hang of living with two more mouths in the house. Mrs. Moore still remembered becoming a new mother when she gave birth to Janet; that is something that a mother never forgets. The Moores went to bed in their new home, and Cliff settled down in his bed, but he could not get to sleep. He was used to having Janet there with him.

The alarm went off at six thirty the next morning, and he slid out of bed and went to the kitchen, naked as usual, to put the coffee on. He had just lowered the water tank cover when someone knocked at the kitchen door. Man, was he glad that they had put a shade on the door and kept it closed. He hollered for them to wait a second, ran back to his bedroom, put on some gym shorts and a T-shirt, and went back to the door.

Opening the door, he found Mr. Moore standing there. "Come on in; you caught me in need of some clothing."

"I just came over to tell you to come over for some breakfast."

"That will be nice, but I will have to eat and run. I need to go into the office before I go to see Janet and the kids."

"Will you and her mother be going over today to see them?"

"I don't know. Her mother hasn't given me my marching orders yet! I don't think we should, but I don't have the deciding vote when it comes to our daughter."

"I understand where you are coming from, Dad, but we let them have their way because we love them. If it was something that we felt we needed to put our foot down over, then we would, but gently, of course."

Mr. Moore smiled and spoke, "Cliff, I see you are learning how to be a good husband. It takes a year or two to know which battles a man should fight with his wife."

"Amen to that one," Clifford replied. "It all comes down to keeping the spouse happy and content."

"Well, I'll go back over and tell Mom that you will be over in a few minutes."

"Okay, I'll go get dressed and be right over."

He went into the bedroom, picked up his cell, and called Janet's number. She answered on the first ring. "Morning, Cliff."

"Morning, Mom. I hope you slept the rest of the night."

"Yes, I was able to get some rest between feeding the babies. I am going to the office this morning, and I will come over after lunch to see you and the kids."

"Man, does that sound nice? I think I am going to love being a dad to these two people that we just brought into this world."

"I think I will love being a mom to them. I know kids can be difficult at times, but that is just part of being a responsible parent."

"I agree," Cliff replied. "I will see you in a few hours. Turn over and get some more sleep."

He finished dressing and went to the Moores' apartment for breakfast.

"I called your daughter before I came over, and she is doing fine and got a few hours of sleep after we left. Daniel and Danielle slept for four hours until they had to be fed and changed. She is breastfeeding, but the nurse changed their diapers. She said the nurse weighed them; Daniel was 7 lbs. 3 oz., and Danielle was 7 lbs. 4 oz."

"That's a good weight for twins," Mrs. Moore told Clifford as she put a plate of breakfast before him. "I don't know if I can eat all of this—three eggs, five pieces of bacon, and three pieces of toast—but I will try."

He gobbled it all down between answering questions that his in-laws asked. "Thanks, but I need to go into the office. Feel free to go see Janet and the kids this afternoon if that's what you decide to do."

He went out the door with a wave of his hand and a goodbye.

Upon pulling into the parking lot of his office, he could see three cruisers sitting in the lot, just as it should be at this time of the day, he thought to himself. Julie buzzed him in as he walked up to the door.

"Morning, Julie. I already called, and Janet and the kids are doing great."

Julie looked surprised. "What do you mean by 'kids'?" she asked.

"You haven't heard?"

"Heard what?" she replied.

"Janet gave birth to twins around two o'clock this morning. We now have a Daniel and a Danielle in our household. Both weigh a little over seven pounds and are doing fine. I will go over this afternoon, but I feel that they will come home tomorrow. The office had planned on giving you two a shower; it looks like it will be a belated one now. At least everyone will know what color to buy."

"Her parents got back from Florida yesterday, and boy, am I glad. I know Janet and I will be able to use the help for a while. They are really happy with their new apartment we had done in the old barn. I imagine her mother will be spending some nights in our house until they can get the babies on a schedule."

"I need to get back and see what is on my desk. Did the captain at the water shed pond call back with any more news?"

"No, I don't think so. I did not take any messages while I was on duty."

He went into his office and started looking at the notes stuck on his desk. Nothing new, just the ones he had left when he had to leave, and as usual, his staff had taken care of putting out the fires. "I need to bring some candy or something as a thank you gesture for the good work these people have done for me."

Ike came in about that time and congratulated Clifford on becoming a daddy. "Two at one time was a real feat in my book."

Each employee on duty came in one by one with their congratulations and best wishes. The phone rang, and he could see it was Captain Jones up at the dam project.

"Morning, Captain. How are things going up at the dam site?"

"Just fine, Sheriff. We will be finishing the repairs on the first one tomorrow and will start to empty the second one the day after. We will be pumping the water from the second pond into the one we just repaired. We hope to save as many fish as we can, but it can't be helped if some of them die; the water has to come out."

"We understand, Captain. I'm sure the Federal Government will restock the ponds when you're done with the repairs."

"Yes, you're right about that, Sheriff. It may take them six months or so, but they will restock them."

"Someone told us this morning while we were eating breakfast at the Pine Stop restaurant that congratulations were in order for you. How are the twins and your wife doing?"

"Fine. I will be going over to see them in a little while. Thanks for the congratulations. Keep me informed of your progress up there."

"Goodbye, Sheriff. I will give you a call once we get started on the other pond."

"Julie, I'm heading into Salem to check on my family."

"That sounds wonderful to me," she spoke. "Yes, it does, Sheriff. Tell them hello for me."

"Sure will." And with that, he got into his cruiser and started to Salem. He walked into Janet's room just as the nurse was placing Danielle in bed with her. Daniel was already laying on one side of her, and now she had Danielle on the other.

"Hi, Mama. How are things going?"

"Just fine." He went over and kissed the mother of his children hard on the mouth.

Chapter Eleven

Clifford went to the hospital the following day and retrieved his wife and their new children. They had purchased the necessary car seat for one baby, so he had to go by the store and pick up another one. To be politically correct, he returned the one he had bought and got a blue one and a pink one, already colour-coding the sex of his kids.

His in-laws were already at their house and ready to take over for their daughter when they arrived home. The in-laws had gone into Roanoke as soon as Clifford had left for work and purchased another bassinet so that everything would be ready when they came home. It was a good thing they had thought of it—Clifford had not considered where the babies would sleep.

Janet sat down in the den, where they had set up both bassinets for the day. The babies were still asleep and didn't realise they had been switched to different beds. The car seats could be used during the day, but their bedroom was just steps away from the kitchen and den, so they could be left in the bedroom for the time being.

Mrs. Moore had decided that she should stay in one of the other bedrooms so she could be in the house at night to help Janet with diaper changes, at least for a few days until she could teach Cliff the art of changing diapers. That was a job he was not thrilled to undertake, but he would step up to the plate and do his duty.

The next day, he went to work after eating the huge breakfast his mother-in-law had prepared for all of them. Of course, she only did breakfast once she had changed the kids' diapers and cleaned them up; after all, she would say, important things first. "Thanks for the breakfast. I need to get to the office. Tell Dad I will see him this evening when I get home," Cliff said as he went out the door.

He drove down the mountain to his office in the courthouse. Things looked quiet when he entered the office, but he had to use his key; Julie was not at her seat when he arrived, but he met her in the hallway on his way to his office.

He finished looking at the paperwork on his desk and had some extra time, so he decided to drive up to the pond and see the progress for himself. Clifford drove up Route 42 and stopped by his home to check on his family. He gave all three of them a kiss on the forehead before leaving; both the kids were asleep and did not wake up even when he kissed them.

Their names were too formal; he and Janet needed to come up with nicknames for each one of them. He didn't think D&D was a good option—it ran them together. Maybe Dan and Dee? He would run this by Janet tonight. He was just about over the curvy mountain road and down to the little country store when he decided to stop by and check on Mary Mann. He went into the store and was pleasantly surprised to find Mary and her grandson behind the counter. He smiled at them both, and they smiled back.

"How are things going for you two?" he asked.

"Just great, Sheriff. My little man here is a lot of help and is doing well in school. He goes to his parents on the weekends to catch up with them, but he likes living here with me, and I hope that continues. But I don't have a say in it. I will do the best I can with him, and my son, who lives in Christiansburg, comes over to check on the two of us. I think this is a good situation for him until his parents get their act together."

He chatted for a while and then said goodbye.

Clifford turned left and drove up to the pond site. When he reached the guard, the guard knew him and motioned for him to go on through. He pulled up to the work trailer just as Captain Jones came out of the door.

He called Jacobs at the FBI in Richmond and was surprised when Jacobs answered instead of his secretary. "Morning, Mr. Jacobs. This is Sheriff Davidson in Craig County. We haven't talked in a while, and I thought I should check in with you about the missing Warren woman. I did check in with our realty company, and the husband did rent a farm in Craig County for a few months, but now no one seems to be able to find out what has happened to him. My deputy and I had lunch with him once a couple of years ago at one of our restaurants, but after that, he has done a disappearing act. Has the FBI found out anything else concerning Charles Warren's whereabouts?"

"No, Sheriff, we haven't had any luck in finding out where he may have gone. I have an uneasy feeling that something has gone awry. It's really weird that Botetourt County cannot find any records whatsoever on this deputy. It's like he was never there and no one cares that he disappeared. I wish there was something else I could do to help you, but I've run out of places and people to ask concerning this guy. I will put out another request for him. We did go to the Social Security board and got all the addresses for him, but none of them have gotten us anywhere."

"Have his in-laws heard from him?"

"No, Sheriff. I called them about a month ago, and they had not heard from their daughter or him. This case is puzzling me. I don't like to have anything like this left unresolved. My re-election is coming up this fall, and if I am not elected, I don't want any unfinished business left for the next person who takes over this office."

"I know how you feel, and I hope something breaks in this case before then."

"Me too. Well, thanks for the information. Keep me in the loop, please. Goodbye."

He finished looking at the paperwork on his desk and had some extra time, so he decided to drive up to the pond and see the progress for himself. Clifford drove up Route 42 and stopped by his home to check on his family. He gave all three of them a kiss on the forehead before leaving; both the kids were asleep and did not wake up even when he kissed them.

Their names were too formal; he and Janet needed to come up with a nickname for each one of them. He didn't think D&D was a good one—it ran them together. Maybe Dan and Dee? He would run this by Janet tonight. He was just about over the curvy mountain road and down to the little country store when he decided to stop by and check on Mary Mann. He went into the store and was pleasantly surprised to find Mary and her grandson behind the counter. He smiled at them both, and they smiled back.

"How are things going for you two?" he asked.

"Just great, Sheriff. My little man here is a lot of help and is doing well in school. He goes to his parents on the weekends to catch up with them, but he likes living here with me, and I hope that continues. But I don't have a say in it. I will do the best I can with him, and my son, who lives in Christiansburg, comes over to check on the two of us. I think this is a good situation for him until his parents get their act together."

He chatted for a while and then told them goodbye.

Clifford turned left and drove up to the pond site. When he reached the guard, the guard knew him and motioned for him to go on through. He pulled up to the work trailer just as Captain Jones came out of the door.

"Morning—or is it afternoon? I've been so busy with government red tape that I've lost track of time."

"Well, it's about two o'clock. I thought I would run up and see how the first pond turned out."

"Sure, come with me, and we'll walk around it. We started yesterday pumping water out of the second one, but it's a slow process and will take us a week or more to drain the pond into this one. As you can see, we've put a vermiculite floor and wall to stabilize the dirt floor and walls. Then we lined the pond with a custom-made vinyl liner. We shouldn't have to do anything to these ponds for many years to come. Once it is drained, we will repair the other pond in the same manner."

"Where will your team go once you have finished here in Craig?"

"We are slated to go up to Mountain Lake and see if we can do anything about it draining down."

"I hope you can. It has always been a nice resort, and with the lake going away, it has hurt the business up there a lot."

"We won't know if there is anything we can do until we take a look at it. It will be a slow go because we will need divers to go down and see what is happening at the bottom. That can be a very risky thing for a diver; he has to make sure the water pull won't suck him into the hole, because if that happened, we would never be able to retrieve him. We hope we can do something about the lake, but it is a natural lake and not man-made. Mother Nature may have her reasons for draining the lake."

Chapter Twelve

Captain Jones finished showing Clifford around the pond, and after he thanked the captain, he headed back to town to his office. It was almost four o'clock by the time he pulled into the parking lot of his office. Looking through the papers, he did not find anything pressing on his desk, so he checked out and went home for the night.

The Moores were at the kitchen table when he went in the back door. Both held a finger up to their mouths to signal him to be quiet and not speak loudly. He knew what was happening and poured himself a cup of coffee, then sat down with them. Janet came into the kitchen, got a cup for herself, and joined them at the table.

"How has everything gone today?" he asked.

"Just fine. Janet got a lot of rest between feedings, and the two of us took on diaper duty and prepared food for the grown-ups. Mom, Dad, you will never know how much Janet and I appreciate you guys helping out. If you hadn't been here to help, I would have had to take a week or two off to help out here."

"Cliff, we are more than happy to help out."

All at once, both babies started crying. "Now what? They were just changed and fed," Janet exclaimed as she got up to attend to them. Clifford picked up Daniel, and Janet reached for Danielle. As soon as they had them in their arms, the babies stopped fussing and went back to sleep. They carried them in their arms and sat down at the table with her parents, holding their children while drinking their coffee. "Now what could be more natural than this?" Clifford said as he smiled and kissed his son on the forehead.

"Now there is a big decision that Janet and I need to make, and you, the Moores, can help us if you like."

"What would that be?" Janet asked.

"We need to pick out a nickname for these kids. I think Daniel and Danielle are just too formal; we need something more loving."

Janet and her parents looked at one another, surprised that Cliff would come up with something like this. Things were quiet at the table for a minute until Janet spoke up. "I agree; we need nicknames that show them we love them dearly. I thought about D&D, but that is just too business-like. I did think that we could call them Dan and Dee. What do you guys think about those names?"

"Dee is alright," Janet interjected, "but I think she should be called Dannie for short."

They all agreed to Dan and Dannie as the children's everyday names. They put Dan and Dannie in their bassinets, and Mrs. Moore put dinner on the table. Clifford was starving, so he was happy to see the food. He would never say it out loud, but Mrs. Moore was a lot better cook than her daughter—maybe that's an acquired skill.

Clifford enjoyed his dinner and volunteered to clean up, but his mother-in-law would not hear of it. "You have worked all day, so I will take care of cleaning up the dishes."

Clifford just raised his arms in surrender. He knew not to argue with a woman when she had made up her mind about how things were going to happen. Mr. Moore and Cliff went into the den, flopped down in recliners, and turned on the evening news. Most of the news was so one-sided politically that he and Janet hardly ever watched it, but he knew Mr. Moore did, so he just went along with watching it for a change.

Later, when the Moores had gone to their apartment, he and Janet retired to their bedroom with their kids. Janet did not want to leave them in another bedroom until they were a few months older. She did not feel good about not being in the same room with her babies at this time.

Cliff understood her feelings; he would have to be a little quiet with his lovemaking. He stripped and went into the shower, and to his surprise, Janet joined him before he could get his washcloth soaped up. She took the cloth from his hand, finished getting it lathered up, and started washing his back. He moaned lightly as she moved her arms and hands around to his chest and washed the nipples of his manly breasts. She moved on down, and then he turned around to face her and pulled her against him. He could feel her hot breasts pressing against his chest.

The way he was holding her, he knew she was more than ready for him to take her body with his. Just as he was about to enter her, the babies started wailing in the other room. Talking about putting a damper on things, Janet wrapped a towel around herself and went to see what the problem was.

Daniel needed a clean diaper, and once that was done, he went back to sleep, and his sister did as well. Cliff was not going to be outdone; he turned off the water until she came back, and they started over. This time, they were able to finish the task at hand.

Clifford awoke the next morning to the clanging of dishes. Mrs.

Moore was already in the kitchen, fixing breakfast. She was adept at multitasking, so she had the bacon frying in the skillet while unloading the dishwasher, which caused the clanging noises. He tried not to wake Janet or the kids when he slid out of bed, easing the bedroom door shut as he left, hoping they would sleep a little longer.

Walking into the kitchen, he gave his mother-in-law a peck on the cheek in appreciation for her help with the kids and them. Mrs. Moore just smiled and said, "Thank you, son. I appreciate your gesture." Cliff reached for the coffee pot and a mug. Pouring himself a cup, he sat down at the table, starting to wake up as soon as the hot coffee hit his tongue. It wasn't long before his father-in-law came through the back door. Cliff put one finger to his lips to signal that the babies were still asleep. Mr. Moore got a mug of coffee and sat down with Cliff at the table, talking in a soft voice.

Mr. Moore was getting bored and wanted to know if there was anything he could do around the place that Cliff hadn't had time to do. "Well, I never got around to putting the siding on the old wood shed behind the barn. I bought the siding, and it's inside the shed. If you feel up to it, you're most welcome to do that chore for me."

Mr. Moore grinned from ear to ear. "I will get on it right after breakfast. Thanks; I needed something constructive to do while we're here."

"This will be a great help, Dad," Cliff said. "One less thing I have to think about. By the way, how long can we count on you two staying here and picking up the slack?"

They both chimed in, "Just as long as you need us and we don't get on each other's nerves."

Clifford smiled and said, "Well, you may want to think about selling that condo in Florida. We could probably use your help for the next eighteen years. It will be that long until we get these two grandchildren of yours out of the house."

The Moores responded, "Well, Cliff, I don't think we can be here quite that long. When the weather turns really cold, I feel like we'll be heading south."

"I was just kidding," Cliff said. "I know you guys want to enjoy your grandchildren and also the warm winter temperatures in Florida."

Janet stumbled out of the bedroom and across the hall into the kitchen just as Cliff had finished talking. "Morning, people. Why didn't you wake me up?"

"We thought you should sleep in with the babies this morning. Grab yourself some coffee; breakfast is almost done, and you'll want to eat yours before those babies start screaming for theirs."

"That's the truth if I ever heard it. Once they get hungry, they don't stop eating until they have every drop of my milk. I'm beginning to wonder if I have enough for the two of them."

Her mom spoke up, "Janet, they look just fine. If they didn't get enough at their feeding, they'd be waking up more often and screaming for more. Mother Nature has a way of training new moms like yourself."

Mrs. Moore put breakfast on the table, and the four of them dug in like starving wolves. They had just finished eating when the kids started howling for theirs. Janet smiled at her mother and went into the bedroom to feed them.

"Well, thanks," Cliff said, "but I need to head to work." He gave them a wave goodbye as he went out the door to his car. His drive down the mountain to the little town of New Castle only took about twenty minutes, but it gave him time to clear his mind of home and get into sheriff mode for his daily responsibilities. Julie buzzed him in the door and said, "Good morning," as he walked by her desk.

"And good morning to you," he replied. "How are those kids doing?"

"Just fine and growing like weeds. They're not a month old and have already doubled their weight."

"Janet says they eat like little pigs."

"Well, she must have good milk if they've put on that much weight," Julie replied.

"Yes," he answered. "She tries to eat right since she's feeding them from her body."

He went back to his office to start his day by clearing yesterday's paperwork away. He had gotten most of it done the day before, so his desktop was clear in just a few minutes. As he looked at the new missing posters that the FBI had sent over, he was surprised to find one for Charles Warren. The FBI had issued the poster because Warren was on the lam and a suspect in his wife's disappearance. Things were really out of order with these two people. Clifford feared that since both were missing, it indicated foul play somewhere along the line.

He decided to walk down Main Street and see who was loafing in town. Today was court day, and a lot of people came just to watch the proceedings. He saw a couple of the older guys who came often, Kenny, Leon, and Calvin, going in the front door as he walked down the hallway to go out.

"Morning, guys. Take care in the courtroom. I wouldn't want the judge to find you in contempt!"

"Yes, Sheriff, we'll be good boys today," they replied. Someone had told him that people like these guys were known as "owls" in the courtroom.

Main Street wasn't more than three blocks long, so it didn't take him long to take his walk. Court didn't start for another twenty minutes, so he took a side street and entered the courthouse through the side entrance. He walked up the long flight of steps to get to the second floor, where the courtroom was located. His deputy was standing at the entrance to the courtroom and turned off the metal detector so he could enter with his revolver strapped to his side. He and his deputies were the only people allowed to be armed while in the courtroom. Taking a seat in the back of the room, he could see any movements that might take place in front of him. This was a small town, but he had learned that small didn't mean something wasn't going to happen.

He looked at the court docket. Most of the items were run-of-the-mill: traffic violations, domestic disputes, and today, a land dispute between the Zimmerman brothers. It seemed one of them claimed their father was to leave the property solely to him and not split it between the two of them because the father had already given the other brother over a hundred thousand dollars to help him start his own business.

The judge ran through all the traffic fines and family disputes. Now it was the brothers' turn to go before the judge. Neither had a lawyer and were going to plead their own cases. The judge listened to what each of them had to say about the property dispute and then made his ruling.

The brother without a signed document from their father stating that the other son wouldn't get any of the property, due to his receiving the other sum of money, was informed that the property was owned by both sons. "It looks like you'll have to buy your brother out if you want all of the property."

Clifford could see the bulge in one son's pant pocket, and when the judge ruled, he saw him putting his hand in his pocket. Clifford knew what was about to happen. He didn't know how the man had gotten a gun into the courtroom, but he was clearly about to use it on his brother—and possibly the judge.

Clifford jumped up and ran to the front of the courtroom, across to where the brother was standing. The man saw Clifford coming and left his hand in his pocket. "Jack, slowly pull your hand out of the pocket," Clifford commanded. The man complied because Clifford already had his revolver out and hanging by his side. He was ready to shoot if necessary.

David Zimmerman did not resist the sheriff. He slowly lifted his hand out of his pocket and placed it behind his back. Clifford handcuffed him and patted him down, pulling out a .38 Special from his front pocket. He looked at the judge and said, "So much for the metal detector at the door." He took David to the holding cell in his office and called the Justice of the Peace to set a bond. Knowing that David wouldn't have the bond money, Clifford arranged for a deputy to take him to the Botetourt County jail to be incarcerated. He hoped the rest of the day would be less eventful.

Julie posted the missing poster of Charles Warren beside that of his wife. Clifford looked at the two posters and felt that something didn't add up. He was concerned that Mr. Warren might have been involved in his wife's disappearance, though he had no concrete evidence to support this. He returned to his office, cleared his desk, and headed home for the night.

When he arrived home, Janet was feeding the children, and her parents were in the kitchen having coffee. Mrs. Moore had prepared her famous spaghetti and garlic bread, with meat sauce simmered for three hours. By the time it was served, Clifford's mouth was watering.

Janet finished feeding the second baby, and Cliff rocked little Dan to sleep while she fed Dannie. Once both babies were settled, they joined the family in the kitchen for the delicious spaghetti and garlic bread. Clifford ate so much he felt miserable, and the discomfort lasted a couple of hours. After her parents cleaned up from supper and headed to their apartment, Janet and Cliff took their showers and went to bed, too full for any fooling around. They kissed each other goodnight and fell asleep.

The next morning, Mrs. Moore came over and made them a good breakfast before delivering some bad news. "Janet, we have enjoyed being here, and our apartment is wonderful, but we both feel it's time to return to Florida for a while."

"I understand," Janet told her mother. "I'll certainly miss you, and I don't mean just for everything you've done for us over the last month or so."

"I know, dear, but it's time for you and Cliff to take over your lives and the kids' lives as well. We'll be leaving tomorrow after we get up, clean the apartment, and close it down. We'll be back in a few months unless you two decide to bring the kids to Florida for a visit, which would be nice."

The next morning, Cliff got up and went to the kitchen, starting the coffee as he had before Mrs. Moore had taken over. He would miss her, but he was looking forward to managing his household, at least for a while. The coffee finished brewing just as the Moores arrived. Janet came into the kitchen as they arrived.

"Mom, do you and Dad want to see your grandchildren before you head out?"

"We'll just look at them," her mother replied. "I don't want them to wake up because we touched them."

"Sit down and have some coffee. If they're not awake by then, you can peek at them before you leave."

"Sounds like a plan to us," her father said as he sat down at the table with his mug of coffee. They drank their coffee, peeked at the babies, and then left to start their journey back to Florida.

Chapter Thirteen

The Moores had been gone for a couple of weeks, and Cliff and Janet had settled into their routine. He would get up, put the coffee on, and get dressed. Janet would prepare his breakfast and send him off to work by eight a.m. Usually, she was lucky, and the twins would sleep until she got the big kid off to work before they started hollering for her attention. She loved her life with Cliff, and motherhood was more than wonderful in her book.

This was how the day began. Cliff had gone to work, and Julie greeted him with a "good morning" when he walked in the door. "So far so good, boss. I got in about seven-thirty to begin my shift, and it has been quiet here."

"Okay, thanks. I hope it stays that way," Cliff replied as he continued to his office.

He entered his office, sat down at his desk, and checked his calendar to see if he had anything important that day. Nothing at all. His day seemed set to be uneventful, just as Julie had said. No sooner had he thought this, when the phone started ringing. It was his private line, so he suspected it might be trouble.

"Morning, Sheriff Davidson speaking. May I help you?"

"Yes, Sheriff. This is Captain Jones at the watershed dam repair. We have removed almost all of the water from the second dam, and a peculiar bundle is starting to show up as the water level drops. Only about half of it is visible, but I'm no policeman, yet it looks very much like a body to me."

"Thank you, Captain. I will be up there as quickly as I can." He hung up and immediately called the FBI office in Roanoke. He knew that Captain Jacobs, who had taken over, was located in Richmond and couldn't get there right away. He dialed the only number he had for the FBI office in Roanoke. After a few rings, Captain Henderson answered.

"Yes, I am Sheriff Davidson in Craig County. I generally work with Captain Jacobs in your Richmond office, but I have an emergency and need some assistance from the FBI right now. I cannot wait for Jacobs to get here from Richmond."

He could sense the silence on the other end of the line. "Well, Sheriff, I'm new here, but I'll call Captain Jacobs and see how he would like me to handle this. Just tell him that the Corps of Engineers has drained the second pond in Craig County, and it looks like we may have a body at the bottom of the pond. Since this is a federal project, it comes under your jurisdiction, not the Sheriff of Craig County's office. My hands will be tied until you get someone over here on-site. I will head up to the pond site and hopefully have someone there within a couple of hours."

"Okay, Sheriff. I will do everything within my power to get someone over there quickly. Thanks. I'm heading up to the pond site right now. The Captain of the Corps needs assistance right away."

Clifford informed Ike about the situation and asked him to man the office while he was gone. Jumping into his cruiser, he sped off, tires screeching as he took off in a hurry. It usually took him about forty-five minutes to reach the ponds, but this morning, he arrived in thirty. The soldier at the entrance waved him through. He stopped at the trailer, and as he got out of his car, he saw several soldiers standing by the second pond. He walked the hundred feet or so to where they were gathered.

Once he reached them, he looked down and saw the item the captain had mentioned. It did look like a body wrapped in something, with the wrapping almost the same colour as the bottom of the pond. Whoever had placed this body there had planned carefully, likely believing the pond would never be drained and the body never found.

"Captain, I have called the FBI; they will be in charge of this since it is a federal project. I can't tell you how long it might take them to get here, but I guess you will have to keep pumping the water out and leave the bundle where it is. The agents will have to deal with it when they arrive on the scene."

Captain Jones agreed and instructed his men to start the pump again, as they had shut it down when the bundle started to appear. Clifford stayed around until the Feds arrived, which ended up being two hours later.

"Morning, Sheriff Davidson. I am Captain Henderson, whom you spoke with on the phone. I called Captain Jacobs, and he told me to take charge of this situation, so here I am. Show me what you were telling me about on the phone."

Captain Jones and Sheriff Davidson took him to the second pond and pointed to the bundle. By now, it was completely above the water that had been covering it.

"I see what you mean; it does resemble a body wrapped in something. I think we'll have to wait until the captain's men finish pumping the water out before we try to recover whatever it is down there."

It took another two hours before all the water was out of the pond. Most of the dirt sides had dried out because the water had been pumped off for a day or two. The FBI had thought to call the coroner to come to the site before leaving the Roanoke area. She arrived about half an hour after Captain Henderson.

"Captain Jones, do you have a machine with a long-armed dipper? We need a couple of your guys, along with me, to walk down the wall and place the bundle in the dipper so it can be brought up from the bottom."

"Yes, sir. I will have the operator bring it around here. Do you and these two men want to head down? I will have the machinery here in a minute."

The two soldiers and the coroner started down the dirt pond wall without too much difficulty. The operator arrived with the machine and lowered the long-armed dipper into the empty pond. They were lucky; the arm was just long enough to reach the bundle at the bottom of the pond. The two soldiers struggled but finally managed to get the bundle into the bucket.

"Get in the bucket, and the operator will bring you back up," Captain Henderson instructed. They followed his suggestion.

When they reached the top, the operator lowered the bucket to the ground, and the soldiers pulled the bundle from it.

"Whatever is wrapped in here feels like it weighs five hundred pounds. It's probably water-logged; it's hard to tell how long it has been at the bottom of this pond."

The coroner began to cut the rope that had been wrapped around the object. Once the ropes were loose, they rolled the object until the wrapping came off. What appeared to be a body was wrapped in an oil tablecloth and taped shut. The water had deteriorated the duct tape, so they removed the tablecloth easily.

Clifford expected to see a woman, namely Mrs. Carla Warren, but instead, he was looking at a man's body. It was so decomposed that he could hardly tell it was male, except for the fact that it was naked and there was one obvious detail.

The coroner said it would take several days to determine the cause of death and identify the body. They loaded the body into the coroner's buggy and took it to the morgue.

Captain Henderson promised Clifford he would keep him in the loop and drove back to Roanoke. Captain Jones had to wait a couple of days so the FBI team could investigate the pond bottom for any additional evidence.

The next day, they found a .45-caliber pistol buried in the mud. Clifford was informed of the pistol recovered by the FBI. It would probably prove to be the murder weapon, but they would have to wait for the full autopsy of the body to confirm the cause of death.

It had been two weeks since the body and gun were found, and Clifford had not heard anything from the FBI concerning them. He had his own thoughts; he knew that the Botetourt County officers carried .45s. He suspected that the body would turn out to be Charles Warren, the missing deputy. He had always thought that the missing wife would be found dead somewhere and that the husband would be the guilty party, but now it seemed that someone else might be involved in this murder.

Several months had passed since Janet's parents had returned to Florida, and she and Clifford had been considering a visit to

Florida with the twins for a week or two, just to get out of Craig County for a while.

Things had been pretty slow in his office, and he figured he could take a break. They called her parents to set up the dates for their visit. Her parents were delighted to have them come and promised to arrange sleeping accommodations for the twins. They had an enclosed sunroom off the living room that could be converted into a bedroom for the twins while they visited.

The Moores rented two small baby beds for the twins to sleep in. They were not walking yet, so they should be easy to confine to a space where they could be watched if their parents went out for the evening. They could hardly wait to see their grandchildren again. Mrs. Moore wondered just how much they had grown since she had left them in Virginia. The twins were starting to eat soft baby food along with their milk and were growing like weeds.

Sunday rolled around, and Clifford had secured the child seats in the back of the truck and packed the necessary items. They were taking the new truck but did not want to fill up the back end with anything that rain could ruin. It was a good thing it was empty because the night before they were to leave, her mother called and asked if they could bring the three-drawer dresser from the spare bedroom, if they weren't using it. They thought they would need it in the sunroom for the twins' clothes, so now it was wrapped in plastic and tied in the back of the truck. He went back into the house, got Dan and she carried Dannie, fastened them in their car seats, and now they were on their way to Florida. The twins were awake when they started, but the motion of the truck soon put them to sleep, hopefully for an hour or two.

They had left early on Sunday morning and planned to drive

straight through to her parents' home. They knew it would be easier on them with the twins to keep on driving and not stop in a hotel room.

Pulling into the parking lot of the condo around eight o'clock that night, they called her dad's cell, and he brought down the small dolly for them to load everything on, including the twins. They were soon up in the condo, and the twins had eaten and were asleep in the rented beds. It had been a long trip, but the four of them made it without too much trouble.

Janet was a little tired and told her parents she was turning in; she needed to stretch out in the bed. She kissed Cliff on the cheek and went into their bedroom. Cliff had to drink a few more cups of coffee to settle down. He had driven all the way and needed to calm his nerves before going to bed.

"Dad, what have you two been doing with yourselves since you came back down to Florida?" Clifford asked.

"Not a lot," her father replied. "We have been enjoying the view and the ocean, and of course, the warm temperatures. We have missed the four of you, but not the cold weather. Has anything happened in that sleepy little town?"

"Well, we have another murder investigation going on right now," Clifford said. "I should say the FBI has the investigation. The watershed ponds at the head of Johns Creek had to be drained and repaired by the Corps of Engineers.

When they drained the second pond, they uncovered a body at the bottom. The FBI is trying to identify the man they found wrapped in a tarp and tablecloth. We had a missing person's photo on file for almost two years, and I thought that was who we were going to find in the wrapped package in the pond. I'm beginning to think that perhaps it is the husband of the missing woman. Both husband and wife are missing."

"I'm starting to think we need to be looking for a living woman, and I think the body is going to turn out to be the husband. He was a Botetourt County deputy, and all of a sudden, Botetourt County has no record of him. They can't find any paperwork on him working for them. I met him at Pine Top a couple of years ago, and he told Ike and me that his wife was in California visiting her parents. Her parents say she never arrived there. I thought maybe he had done away with the wife and then disappeared, but it looks like it might have been the other way around. I won't know anything more until we get back to Virginia and I talk with the FBI captain in charge of the case."

"I need to go to bed. Thanks for the coffee. I'll see you in the morning."

"Good night, Cliff. See you in the morning."

He took his clothes off and slid between the sheets next to Janet. He could hear her snoring lightly. He knew she was tired and didn't wake her.

He awoke to the sound of babies crying and jumped out of bed, running into the sunroom where the babies were.

Unfortunately, he didn't think about how he was dressed—or rather, how he was not dressed. He always slept in the nude, and he had run to the babies naked. He and Mrs. Moore reached the babies at the same time.

"I've got them, Cliff. I think you need to go put something on to cover that monster," Mrs. Moore said.

He realized then how he was not dressed and turned, walking quickly back to his bedroom. Janet was awake now, and he told her what had happened. She snickered and got up to tend to the kids. Her mother thought it was pretty funny but commented to her daughter that she understood why she had married him now.

Janet blushed but did not say anything to her mother; she just picked up one of the crying babies and started feeding the child. Cliff went into the dining room the next morning rather sheepishly, but his mother-in-law did not mention the incident. He breathed a sigh of relief, silently thanking Mrs. Moore for not saying anything about last night.

"Guys, what do you want to do today?" Mr. Moore asked. "We can keep Dan and Dannie if the two of you want some time to yourselves."

Cliff and Janet looked at each other and both said, "OK," at the same time. "I guess that settles it, Mom. We have the kids today so the young people can take the day off from parenting."

The four of them had a wonderful breakfast, and then Janet and Cliff got in the car and drove north on A1A. They pulled into a beach outlet close to the FPL energy plant and started walking down the path toward the beach.

When they got to the beach, they were surprised to see naked bodies lying on the sand. They just kept walking down the shoreline, keeping their eyes forward, until they passed the people sunbathing in the nude.

Once they were further down the beach, they decided, why not? It seemed natural to them. They peeled off their clothes and used them to sit on; they didn't want sand in their cracks, pardon the pun. They played in the ocean naked and laid on their clothes to soak up the sun.

A couple of hours later, they put their clothes back on and returned to their truck. They both agreed they would not tell her parents about this trip; it would be something to keep to themselves.

They enjoyed the week they spent with her parents, and Cliff gained five pounds eating all the food his mother-in-law prepared. They kissed her parents goodbye and headed back to Virginia.

The kids were really good on the trip back, sleeping most of the time and only waking up to be fed and changed into dry diapers. They were old enough now and taking bottles of formula and soft baby food, so they were a little easier to handle. Cliff could feed Dan while Janet took care of Dannie.

The truck handled the trip well, and they did not have any trouble with it, which was expected since it was almost new with very few miles on it.

Chapter Fourteen

They reached their Virginia home late that night after driving straight through for eleven hours. He had to admit that he had broken the law by driving much faster than the posted speed limit. The alarm went off, and he felt as if he had just put his head on his pillow.

Slipping out of his side of the bed, he went to the kitchen and put on the coffee. He quietly returned to the bedroom, went to the shower, stepped in, and started to soap up his tired body. Janet opened the shower door, stepped in, took his washcloth, and started washing his back.

"I know we don't have time to fool around, but I wanted to start your day off right for you," she said.

"Thank you. I think you may have just started something I will want every morning," he replied.

"Don't count on it," she said, just as the twins started crying.

He went to town after having a couple of cups of coffee, stopping by the quick-stop market for a sausage biscuit to take to work with him. Julie buzzed him in and greeted him with a hand wave and a welcome back.

"How are things in Florida?" she asked.

"Just great. How about here? Anything I need to know about right away?"

"Nah, things have been quiet around here, but I'm sure with you back, things will pick up. They always do!"

He smiled and went to his office to start sorting through the sticky notes. Nothing but normal stuff, which the deputies had taken care of for him. He went to the breakroom, got a cup of coffee, heated his biscuit in the microwave, and returned to his desk to eat his breakfast. While chewing on the biscuit, he couldn't help but think of how much better his mother-in-law's breakfast was.

He had swallowed the last bite when his phone began to ring. Picking it up, he swallowed one last gulp and said, "Sheriff Davidson speaking."

"Morning, Sheriff. This is Captain Jacobs from the FBI office in Richmond, Virginia."

"Yes, Captain, I remember you. What can I do for you this morning?"

"I'm just calling to update you on the body that was found in the watershed pond a month or so ago."

"Yes, I was wondering when I might hear from you guys concerning this case."

"I have two things to tell you. Number one, the body is beyond identifying, but the gun has been traced to the Botetourt County Sheriff's Department. They could not find where it was assigned to a deputy,

but it was in their inventory of weapons."

"That leaves us nowhere, I would say," Cliff spoke.

"I hate to say it, but I think you're correct."

"Captain, I'm sure the FBI is putting together their own theories about the case, but here's what I think: There has been a missing persons poster out for Carla Warren, the missing wife of a Botetourt County Deputy, who is also missing. I think the FBI has been looking for the wrong spouse. I believe the body found is Deputy Warren and we need to be looking for his wife as a suspect in his murder."

"You could be right, Sheriff, but we don't have anything concrete to go on. The deputy lived in your county and, as you know, he moved and left no forwarding address. The Botetourt County Sheriff's Department can't confirm he was a deputy because all the paperwork is missing. You're between a rock and a hard place, as the old saying goes."

"Thanks for the information. If I find anything on this end, I'll give you a call in Richmond."

He ended the call and went back to looking through the pile of papers on his desk, most of which were for his review before Julie could file them away. Whoever said that when computers were invented we would go paperless was wrong. He finished up that pile, walked over to Julie's desk, and put them in her file box. She was coming back from the breakroom with a cup of coffee in her hand.

"Thanks a heap," she said.

"You're welcome," Clifford replied.

He would have liked to call Janet to see how things were going, but he was afraid the twins might be asleep and he might wake them. Just then, the phone rang, and he saw it was Janet calling. He picked up the phone and asked if everything was okay.

"Yes, Cliff. I just thought I'd check in. This morning was weird, and both of us were sort of tired."

"Not much going on here. I'll let you finish that backwash tonight."

Janet was silent for a few seconds before replying, "It's your turn to wash my back."

"That's a go," Cliff replied. "But I won't stop with just your back, so beware, my woman!"

She just kissed him over the phone and hung up.

Ike came into Clifford's office after lunch, and they discussed the body and gun that had been discovered in the pond. Ike agreed that Clifford's theory seemed the most logical. Once he had told Clifford that, the theory started Clifford thinking about the case all over again.

"We can't waste too much time. It's in the hands of the FBI right now, but do keep your mind on it and let me know if you have any odd thoughts about this case."

"I sure will, but right now, I can't think of anything else." Ike got up and went out to his desk, starting to read the newspaper. He didn't have to go on his rounds in the county for another hour.

Clifford's phone began to ring, and he picked it up. Before he could say anything, a man's voice came on the line.

"Sheriff, do you know about the Dead Man's Cavern over on the fields of the Sizer farm?"

"No, I don't think I've heard of it. But go on."

"The opening is on the Sizer farm on Big Mountain Road. You'll know the farm; it's about a mile from Forty-Two and has lots of old junk cars around the farmhouse. The cavers from VPI are allowed to go into this cavern, and they say it runs a long way under the land on Meadow Creek. The guys say you can see well pipes running down through it when you explore. Anyway, I was talking to a group of four students who had just come up from the cavern, and they told me to call you. They think there might be a body down about fifty feet, where it levels off and starts running along with the flat land above."

"Thanks. May I ask who I'm speaking with?"

"I'd rather not get involved. I just wanted to pass along what I was told."

"That's okay. Thanks for the tip. I'll have someone look into it right away."

Clifford sat at his desk, wondering what to do next. He knew for sure he wasn't going down into the cavern, and he didn't think the deputies would either. He picked up the phone and dialled Captain Jacobs's number in Richmond. Jacobs picked up on the second ring.

"Clifford, what do I owe this call so soon after our last one?"

"It's like this—I'm in a pickle and think you might be able to help me out."

Jacobs started laughing. "Okay, spill it, Clifford."

"We have reports of a body in a fifty-foot cavern, and I need a team of professional cavers to go down, find it, and bring it back up to the top."

"That shouldn't be a problem, Clifford. Let me call the Roanoke office and see what I can dig up for you. I'll call you back in a few minutes."

"Thanks, I'll be waiting for your call."

It seemed like an eternity, but it was only about twenty minutes before Jacobs called back.

"I have a team on their way to your office right now. Give them about an hour."

"I sure will. Thanks so much for the help in this matter."

"No problem, Clifford."

Jacobs hung up, and Clifford waited impatiently for the team to arrive.

The team of three young men arrived, and Clifford led them up the mountain to the farm. Ike knew where the cavern was located, so he had already cleared everything with the landowner and was waiting at the gate where they needed to turn into the field. Ike was in a four-wheel drive truck, and they loaded up in it and he drove them and their equipment to where the cavern opened up.

"I was told there is what looks like a body about fifty feet below the surface in this cavern. Please find it and bring what you find up to the top for us to examine."

"Yes, sir, we'll go down now. I don't think it will take us more than twenty minutes to do this. I have a cell phone, but I'm not sure if I'll get a signal while we're underground. We'll wait for a call or you popping up out of the ground."

The team had been underground for about an hour when the leader came up to the surface.

"We found something wrapped up down there. It appears to be too small for a man. I will hook up this hoist over the hole so we can bring whatever it is up to the surface."

Once the hoist was in place, he lowered the rope attached to it down the hole, and within ten minutes, they were pulling the object out of the hole and laying it on the ground. Clifford had called the funeral home to send a hearse, as they did not have a coroner in the county. Clifford and Ike unrolled the carpet slowly, and when it was all unrolled, there lay a woman's body, very badly decomposed.

He pulled out his cell phone and dialled Captain Jacobs's number.

"Jacobs, this is Clifford. We have a very badly decomposed woman's body here. If I don't miss my guess, it will turn out to be Carla Warren. Do you want to send your coroner over, and we won't handle it anymore?"

"The team you sent said they had inspected the site where they found the body, and there was nothing but the body in the cavern."

"Just hold the body where you have it, and I will have the Roanoke office pick it up. This puts a twist on this situation. If the male body is Deputy Warren and this is his wife, then who killed them both?"

"I don't know, Captain. I hope the FBI can find something on this body to help with this case or find some way to identify the male body positively."

"I hope so too, Clifford. This case is beginning to stink, as far as I'm concerned."

The coroner arrived at the scene in an hour and a half. His vehicle was a four-wheel drive, so he came through the field to the cavern, known in the county as The Murder Hole. The legend was that a peddler was murdered and his wagon and the peddler were put in the hole. Neither was ever found in the cavern. The coroner gave a quick look and said, "It's a female, but that's all I can tell you right now."

He loaded the body into his van and went back to Roanoke. He said that his boss would let Clifford know what they found out from the examination of the body. Everyone left the farm, and Clifford went to the owner's house to notify him of what had been found.

Chapter Fifteen

Clifford sat at his desk, wondering what to do next. He knew for sure he wasn't going down into the cavern, and he didn't think the deputies would either. He picked up the phone and dialled Captain Jacobs's number in Richmond. Jacobs picked up on the second ring.

"Clifford, what do I owe this call so soon after our last one?"

"It's like this—I'm in a pickle and think you might be able to help me out."

Jacobs started laughing. "Okay, spill it, Clifford."

"We have reports of a body in a fifty-foot cavern, and I need a team of professional cavers to go down, find it, and bring it back up to the top."

"That shouldn't be a problem, Clifford. Let me call the Roanoke office and see what I can dig up for you. I'll call you back in a few minutes."

"Thanks, I'll be waiting for your call."

It seemed like an eternity, but it was only about twenty minutes before Jacobs called back.

"I have a team on their way to your office right now. Give them about an hour."

"I sure will. Thanks so much for the help in this matter."

"No problem, Clifford."

Jacobs hung up, and Clifford waited impatiently for the team to arrive.

The team of three young men arrived, and Clifford led them up the mountain to the farm. Ike knew where the cavern was located, so he had already cleared everything with the landowner and was waiting at the gate where they needed to turn into the field. Ike was in a four-wheel drive truck, and they loaded up in it and he drove them and their equipment to where the cavern opened up.

"I was told there is what looks like a body about fifty feet below the surface in this cavern. Please find it and bring what you find up to the top for us to examine."

"Yes, sir, we'll go down now. I don't think it will take us more than twenty minutes to do this. I have a cell phone, but I'm not sure if I'll get a signal while we're underground. We'll wait for a call or you popping up out of the ground."

The team had been underground for about an hour when the leader came up to the surface.

"We found something wrapped up down there. It appears to be too small for a man. I will hook up this hoist over the hole so we can bring whatever it is up to the surface."

Once the hoist was in place, he lowered the rope attached to it down the hole, and within ten minutes, they were pulling the object out of the hole and laying it on the ground. Clifford had called the funeral home to send a hearse, as they did not have a coroner in the county. Clifford and Ike unrolled the carpet slowly, and when it was all unrolled, there lay a woman's body, very badly decomposed.

He pulled out his cell phone and dialled Captain Jacobs's number.

"Jacobs, this is Clifford. We have a very badly decomposed woman's body here. If I don't miss my guess, it will turn out to be Carla Warren. Do you want to send your coroner over, and we won't handle it anymore?"

"The team you sent said they had inspected the site where they found the body, and there was nothing but the body in the cavern."

"Just hold the body where you have it, and I will have the Roanoke office pick it up. This puts a twist on this situation. If the male body is Deputy Warren and this is his wife, then who killed them both?"

"I don't know, Captain. I hope the FBI can find something on this body to help with this case or find some way to identify the male body positively."

"I hope so too, Clifford. This case is beginning to stink, as far as I'm concerned."

The coroner arrived at the scene in an hour and a half. His vehicle was a four-wheel drive, so he came through the field to the cavern, known in the county as The Murder Hole. The legend was that a peddler was murdered and his wagon and the peddler were put in the hole. Neither was ever found in the cavern. The coroner gave a quick look and said, "It's a female, but that's all I can tell you right now."

He loaded the body into his van and went back to Roanoke. He said that his boss would let Clifford know what they found out from the examination of the body. Everyone left the farm, and Clifford went to the owner's house to notify him of what had been found.

Cliff spoke up and said, "I think I'm going to order the roasted chicken with wild rice. For some reason, that sounds good to me tonight. The oven-baked apples sound yummy, and a tossed salad to go with it. I think I'll have the same."

Janet replied, "I'll have the same."

The server returned with their wine and asked if they were ready to order or if they would like an appetizer before dinner.

"We'll skip the appetizer and we're ready to order. She and I will have the roasted chicken on wild rice, with a tossed salad and roasted apples as side dishes."

Robert took their orders and excused himself to put them in the kitchen.

"Hmm, this wine is wonderful. It's hard to find a great-tasting white wine," Janet remarked.

Cliff agreed, "The wine is good, but I'm having to take sips when I just want to gulp it down. It's so pleasing to my palate."

When their meal arrived, Cliff had already finished his glass, so he asked for coffee to have with his meal. Janet still had the wine, so she didn't want any other drink with her meal. They were hungry after their room exercises and began eating. They both looked up, commented on how hungry they were, and smiled at one another. Cliff winked at her, knowing exactly what she meant.

This man had become her world, now only second to her children. Children are the number one priority in both parents' lives; they would gladly jump in front of a bus to save their child if necessary. Cliff and Janet still had that haunting desire for one another, even with the kids around. They just couldn't display it in every room of the house.

They finished their meal and declined dessert, feeling full and not wanting to push the feeling—after all, they might need to exercise later. Walking down the street back to their hotel, they were content and feeling great. He had his arm around her waist, and they walked at a slow pace.

Clifford could hear footsteps behind them, and the footsteps were keeping up with their slow pace. "Janet, just keep walking as we are, but I'm going to take my arm from around your waist. It may not be anything, but there is a person behind us, and I want to be ready if they try something."

He removed his arm from her waist, and they continued walking. The person behind them spoke up, "Stop walking and turn slowly around to face me."

Cliff and Janet stopped and turned as requested. Clifford saw a police officer standing there, grinning like a possum.

"John, what on earth are you doing here?" Clifford asked.

"I wanted to live in a warmer climate, so I came down here on vacation. The police force needed an officer, so I applied and got the job. I was walking behind you and kept thinking it had to be you in front of me."

"John Elmore, this is my wife Janet. Janet, John is one of my training buddies from the state police academy."

They talked for a while and decided to meet John and his wife, Joan, at the Hideaway the following night for dinner at seven o'clock. They shook hands and went their separate ways—John to his walking beat and the Davidsons to their hotel room.

It was ten o'clock by now, and both Janet and Cliff were pretty tired. When they got back to the room, they phoned her parents to check on the kids and then hit the hay. Clifford's alarm on his watch woke them at nine a.m. They had slept all night long and had not awakened to use the bathroom. He went to the bathroom as soon as he got out of bed and took care of things. He returned to the bedroom, and Janet was getting out of bed.

"What are you doing up, honey?" he asked.

"Well, dear, when it sounds like a horse peeing in the bathroom, it sort of wakes you up from a sound sleep."

"I'm sorry. Next time, I'll shut the door and try not to groan when I pee."

Janet went into the bathroom to take care of things, and Cliff lay back down on the bed, naked, of course. When she came back into the bedroom, she could tell he was in the mood; his member was up and ready for action. They enjoyed one another for an hour or so and then went out for breakfast.

The little open café was wonderful. Janet just wanted some ice-cold fruit and a bagel with hot coffee for her breakfast. On the other hand, Clifford was starving and ordered three eggs over easy, two sausage patties, a bowl of strawberries, grits, and sausage gravy on biscuits. By the time they had slowly eaten their breakfasts, they were full. The beach was right there, so they decided on a two-mile walk on the beach that morning. The ocean was the most beautiful blue, clear enough to see the bottom, at least where they ventured into the water. They wore shorts, not bathing suits, so they had to watch to avoid getting wet from the incoming waves, not that it would have mattered if they had. They enjoyed their peaceful walk down the beach; everyone they met spoke to them. This just goes to show you, not everyone is snobbish and stuck up. It never hurts to smile at a stranger; you never know what they might be going through, and you could help brighten their day.

The beach walk was wonderful, but it meant another shower. Janet thought Cliff would probably want another romp, but he surprised her. When he came out of the shower, he didn't seem up for it. She didn't say anything, just got dressed in some clean shorts and a top.

"What now, big boy?" she called out to Clifford.

"How about touring the Ernest Hemingway House? The author lived in the Keys during the 1930s and liked cats. It is said he had as many as 150 cats between his homes in Key West and Cuba. There are still around 56 cats at his house and museum in Key West, Florida."

"Okay, let's go," Janet replied. "It's only about ten minutes from here. We could walk if you want to."

"That sounds like a good idea to me. I think I gained ten pounds at dinner last night. We'll have to go lighter tonight when we order."

The walk to the Hemingway House and Museum was a beautiful outing, though it turned out to be a half-hour walk, not ten minutes

. Janet didn't mind; it was 75 degrees and sunny—perfect weather for a walk. The museum was very interesting and covered everything about Hemingway. The cats were special; some had as many as nine toes on their front paws, while a normal cat has only five. All the cats had four toes on their back paws, which is the usual number.

It was mid-afternoon by the time they returned to their hotel, and they were a bit tired from all the walking—first down the beach, then to Hemingway's place. When they got to their room, they both flopped on the bed for a quick nap before dinner. Janet woke up around four o'clock and saw that Cliff was still snoring, so she turned over and went back to sleep.

The next thing she heard was Cliff's voice saying, "Janet, wake up. It's six o'clock, and we're supposed to meet John and his wife at seven at the Hideaway." He had already cleaned up and dressed, so she had the bathroom to herself. Throwing her dirty clothes on the bathroom floor, she jumped into the shower. It didn't take her two minutes—more of a rinse-and-go than a real shower. "Thank goodness my hair is still okay. The wind didn't make it greasy or messy." All she had to do was dress and straighten her hair a bit.

When she was ready, Cliff looked at her and said, "You look like a million dollars."

"Thanks so much, doll. You clean up pretty nicely yourself."

He gave her a big hug and a sloppy kiss, and they went out the door to meet John and his wife.

Chapter Sixteen

It was close, but they walked up to the front door of the restaurant just as John and Joan approached.

"John, you've met my wife, Janet. Janet, this is John's wife, Joan. I'm Clifford, your husband's buddy from the academy," Clifford introduced.

Everyone exchanged pleasantries, and then all four went into the Hideaway. The same hostess from the night before seated them and informed them that Robert would be their server. She left them with their menus and departed. No sooner had she left than Robert arrived to take their drink orders. John and Joan knew Robert; he was a neighbour and a college student working to save money for his bills.

"Robert, there will be one check, and it's mine. My wife and I are treating old friends to dinner tonight," Clifford said.

John started to object, but Clifford cut him off. "No, John, it's our treat."

John didn't argue further. Clifford began the conversation by sharing that he and Janet had two boys and a girl: twins Dannie, a girl, and Danny, a boy, who were five years old, and a two-year-old boy named James Francis. He was the Sheriff of Craig County and had been for fifteen years.

"Your turn, John. How long have you and Joan been married?"

"This year will be our fifth wedding anniversary, and we have a little girl named Amanda. She's two years old and the apple of her Daddy's eye," Joan chimed in.

"Of course, that's just the way it is with daddies and daughters," Janet added.

They enjoyed a wonderful dinner together. Janet and Cliff both had steak dinners, while John and Joan ordered the chicken dinners that Janet and Cliff had enjoyed the night before. They had warned John and Joan that each dinner would be enough for two people, but they didn't listen and ended up with doggie bags as the four of them walked out of the restaurant.

John and Clifford were shaking hands when a loud Ford Mustang drove by. The women were standing beside their husbands when a loud noise went off. It sounded like the car backfired, but when Clifford turned around, he saw Joan lying on the sidewalk.

They were all stunned, but Clifford leaped into action. "John, call for an ambulance now," he ordered, and then he got down beside Joan and examined her. He saw blood oozing from her chest above one of her breasts.

"John, I think it's a gunshot wound. Do you have a handkerchief I can use to stop the bleeding?"

"I have some tissues in my purse," Janet said as she opened her bag and pulled them out.

He took the tissues, unbuttoned Joan's blouse, and saw where the bullet had entered her chest. He applied pressure with the tissues to the wound and held the makeshift bandage in place until the medics arrived. He explained the situation to them, and they took over from there. John went with Joan to the hospital, while Janet and Clifford answered the police officer's questions.

The officer could hardly grasp the situation when Clifford

provided a description of the car and its license number. The two men in the car were Asian-looking and in their early twenties. Clifford identified himself as the Sheriff of Craig County, Virginia, and a former Virginia State Trooper.

The officer thanked him for the information and took his personal details in case they needed to contact him later.

As soon as they were through with the officer, they went to the hospital to check on Joan. The clinic on the island was very small, but they did have an MD on call when Joan arrived. He examined her and had an X-ray done of her upper chest area where the bullet had entered. She had been lucky; the bullet had missed any bones and exited through her back. She was awake when she arrived at the clinic and had been given something to sedate her slightly during the examination.

The wound was clean, front and back; they cleaned and bandaged the areas and gave her some mild pain medication before sending her home with instructions to return in two days to ensure no infection set in.

Janet and Clifford had to leave the next day to return to Port Saint Lucie to pick up the kids and then head back to New Castle. The next morning, Clifford called John to check on Joan. She had slept all night and awoke with only a sore shoulder. They felt she had been fortunate; had the bullet struck her heart, the outcome could have been dire. Clifford gave John his cell phone number and asked him to keep them updated on Joan's progress. John agreed and thanked Clifford for his assistance, mentioning that it was a drive-by shooting as he knew of no one who would want either him or Joan harmed. Clifford wished him and Joan well, then turned to Janet. "It's time, dear. We need to pack up and head home. It's been nice, but it's time to pay the piper and return to work."

They packed up the truck and headed off the island, taking Interstate 95 to pick up the children at her parents' place. Once out of Miami, the traffic thinned out somewhat but was still dense enough that Clifford had to watch carefully for reckless drivers speeding and weaving through the six lanes of traffic. It took them about six hours to reach Port St. Lucie, where her parents lived on Hutchinson Island.

As they reached the Intracoastal Waterway bridge leading to the island, it wasn't much farther to her parents' condo. When they walked in the front door, their three children nearly knocked them down as they rushed for hugs and kisses. The parents were equally glad to see their kids, realising just how much they had missed them. After the hugs and kisses, the four adults sat down at the kitchen table for some coffee.

"Mom and Dad, we appreciate you taking care of the children. We needed this time away for the two of us," Janet said.

Her mother responded, "Darling daughter, your father and I were young and in our prime once too. We understand all about children and how they can put a damper on your adult love life," she said with a grin and wink. After all, she had seen Clifford in the buff and knew what her daughter was receiving from her husband. "We'll spend the night and then pack up and try to leave early in the morning, but with three kids, I expect it'll be more like mid-morning before you get on the road."

The next morning, Mrs. Moore woke Janet at 7 a.m. as she had asked her to, if she was up before them. "Thanks, Mom. I'll get the family up and going," Janet replied. While Janet got her children out of bed, her mother started breakfast. She knew Janet and her family ate well and wanted to send them off with full stomachs. When Clifford and his family reached the breakfast table, it was loaded with food: sausage gravy on homemade biscuits, scrambled eggs, applesauce, and bacon.

"Mom, I won't be able to drive after eating all of this," Clifford said.

"I'm sure you'll manage, Cliff," she replied.

They ate, packed, and left, with Mrs. Moore insisting that Janet not worry about changing the beds or cleaning up the dishes. "I'll have all day to handle those things after you hit the road back to New Castle."

4o mini

Chapter Seventeen

It was almost 10 a.m. before they were able to leave Port St. Lucie and get on the road home. "Janet, we'll have to play it by ear and see if we can make it home today, but it'll be after midnight before we get to New Castle, or maybe later. It just depends on the traffic and if we run into any delays," Clifford said.

"I know, honey. I can drive some of the way, just let me know when you want me to," Janet replied.

"I will, honey. I trust you driving in this traffic; you're a pretty good defensive driver," Clifford said.

They had already traveled for two hours up I-95, and the kids were all asleep in the back seat. Janet hoped the movement of the truck would keep them asleep for a few more hours. The sign read "Jacksonville 23 miles," and it was almost noon. The traffic would be thick, but not as bad as the 5 o'clock traffic in the city. Clifford decided to take I-95 through Jacksonville instead of the 295 bypass. If traffic was heavy, the wrap-around was easier than navigating through the city. They made it through without any problems, avoiding the stop-and-go traffic that sometimes resulted from accidents.

Janet was relieved to be past Jacksonville; she hated the traffic there more than anywhere else. Clifford didn't seem to mind; he kept a smile on his face and his hands on the wheel, blending in with the other cars. His years in law enforcement had prepared him for navigating traffic. They were now headed toward Savannah, Georgia. It would be quite late by the time they reached the outskirts, so they planned to stop for dinner with the kids. Her mother had packed them a basket of food and drinks, so they stopped at a rest area for a picnic before continuing.

As they neared Savannah, they took the Green Spring exit and stopped at Shoney's. It took a while to feed the kids and get them back into the truck. It was now 6 p.m., and they still had another eight hours to go.

"Cliff, how about I start driving now? The kids are asleep, and you can get some rest. Maybe we can make it home tonight if you get some sleep now," Janet suggested.

"Honey, that sounds like a good plan to me," Clifford agreed. He pulled over to the shoulder and slightly onto the grass to switch drivers. The kids slept through the process, and Clifford reclined his seat and started snoring. Janet hoped he wouldn't wake them with his noise. She had punched him many times in their married life to get him to stop snoring.

Janet made good time, speeding a bit more while Clifford slept. She took the exit off I-95 North onto I-26 West, which would lead them to I-77 North. The family didn't wake when she slowed for the exit, so she accelerated back to 85 mph.

Suddenly, blue lights started flashing behind them. "Oh crap, Cliff won't like this," Janet muttered. "Cliff, wake up," she said, giving him a nudge as she signaled and pulled to the side of the road. Clifford sat up, his senses returning as he saw the blue lights.

"How fast were you going?" he asked Janet as the officer approached.

"I was doing 85 when he turned his lights on," Janet replied.

"Okay, let me handle this," Clifford said, pulling out his wallet with his badge. "He'll want to see your driver's license, Janet."

Janet had already taken her license out. When the officer, a woman, approached the truck window, Janet rolled it down and handed over both her license and Clifford's badge. "I'm sorry, officer. I know I was speeding. We're trying to get back to Virginia tonight. My husband has to be back on the job tomorrow." It was a small fib, but she hoped it might help her avoid a ticket.

The officer took their license back to her cruiser, and Clifford knew she was running a check on them. When she returned, she shook her finger at Janet. "Young lady, you need to ease up on the gas pedal. I'm going to just warn you this time, but don't let me catch you going 85 in South Carolina again."

"Yes, ma'am. I'll slow it down," Janet promised.

"I can start driving now since you've gotten us pulled over," Clifford said.

Janet smiled, "I've made good time and we should be able to get home before it gets very early in the morning."

"Yes, dear, I'll give you that. We are ahead of schedule, but you've woken the three munchkins in the back seat." The twins were doing okay, but James Francis was starting to cry and cause problems. They were lucky; there was a rest area just ahead. Clifford took the exit, and Janet gave the children some juice and calmed James Francis down.

Janet could tell that Cliff wasn't angry about her being stopped for speeding. He had been stopped before himself. He generally kept it under the eighty-mark, but sometimes, if he was in a hurry, he would put the hammer down. She worked with James Francis and got him back to sleep at the rest area. The twins were thirsty and had something to drink, and now they were asleep again due to the movement of the truck as they went down the road.

They had just taken the on-ramp onto Interstate 77 in South Carolina. This would lead them through North Carolina and into Virginia. There were still about seven hours left to drive, but they would get there sometime around 2 a.m., depending on the traffic conditions they encountered on the rest of the way home.

Clifford would probably drive the rest of the way home since he had gotten a nap and was now in good shape. Janet planned to try to get a nap just in case he got sleepy and she needed to take over the driving. He had been driving for an hour on I-77, and the traffic was light, making for an easy drive. Charlotte, North Carolina, would be coming up in another hour or so, and it didn't matter what time of day or night you went through; traffic was always heavy, and you had to watch out.

Things went well for the next hour or so, but the traffic began to thicken as they entered Charlotte. The kids and Janet were still asleep, which he was thankful for. He was halfway through Charlotte when traffic came to a halt. It was midnight, and he hadn't seen any signs indicating road work. He finally reached a police car directing traffic to take the bypass due to an accident on the road. He followed the signs, and the delay added no more than twenty minutes to their trip. He was finally getting out of the Charlotte area, and traffic was starting to move faster. Another half-hour and they would reach the Virginia state line, with about three more hours left on the trip.

Janet awoke and asked quietly where they were, not wanting to wake the kids. They had a thermos of coffee that they had filled a few hundred miles back when they refueled the truck. She poured him a sippy cup full of warm coffee; it wasn't really hot, but he drank coffee at various temperatures. He had a reputation around Craig County for being a serious coffee drinker. She had meant to buy one of those thermoses that plug into the truck to keep beverages warm.

He thanked her for the coffee and patted her on the leg. She reached over, kissed him on the cheek, and put her hand on his member, telling him she would take care of things tomorrow. It didn't excite Cliff this time; he was tired and focused on driving. She hadn't meant to excite him, just to wake him up a bit. He felt the tingling but refused to let it become a distraction.

Janet went back to sleep after pouring his coffee and settled into her seat. Clifford finished the trip without any mishaps. He pulled into their driveway right at 2 o'clock. He would unload the truck tomorrow after resting a few hours. For now, he helped Janet get the kids into the house and into their beds. He was glad to drop his clothes on the floor beside the bed and crawl in between the sheets. Janet was happy just to snuggle up against him and go to sleep. Her hot body against his had him stiff as a board, but he was too tired to act on it. He shut his eyes tight and fell asleep.

Janet woke around 8:30 a.m. The few hours of sleep had rested her, and when she opened her eyes, she saw that Cliff was already out of bed. Rolling out of bed and throwing on a robe, she went to the kitchen, but Cliff wasn't there. Stepping to the kitchen door, she saw him coming up the walk with items he was bringing from the truck. She opened the door for him once he had come up the steps onto the porch and took one or two items from him.

"Honey, you should have waited for me to help you. That would be nice, but you'll have your hands full when the kids wake up."

He had hardly spoken these words when the twins came into the kitchen, yawning. "Breakfast will be a while. You munchkins go to the bathroom and wash your face and hands."

Chapter Eighteen

Janet prepared breakfast for all the children, including the one she had slept with. He swallowed it whole, gave her a peck on the cheek, and headed down to New Castle to his office. The drive down the mountain was uneventful, but as he pulled into the parking lot of his office, he saw an FBI vehicle already parked.

Julie buzzed him in when he approached the door and informed him that an FBI agent from the Roanoke office was waiting for him in his office.

Clifford went to his office, and the agent stood up, shook his hand, and introduced himself. "I'm Ben Eckard from the regional office in Roanoke, Virginia."

"Have a seat, Ben. Would you like a cup of coffee or water?"

"No thanks, Sheriff. I just had breakfast before I came across the mountain to talk with you."

"Well, what can I do for you, Ben?"

"It's like this, Sheriff. Just call me Clifford; everyone else does."

"Okay, Clifford. It seems we have a problem. The police in Key West, Florida, have arrested the two men who were driving the Mustang that shot your friend's wife last week."

"Yes, my wife and I were with them when it happened."

"The facts are, they were aiming at you, but you made a quick movement just as the guy pulled the trigger, and he hit your friend's wife instead. They have confessed to the shooting and also that they were hired by someone. They didn't have a name for him;

I can see why he wouldn't tell them if he was orchestrating a murder. We have a composite sketch of what he looks like, based on their descriptions."

Ben pulled out the sketch and showed it to Clifford. Ben could see the surprise on Clifford's face, followed by a smile.

"I knew it from the start, and this proves it!" Clifford said.

"Proves what?" Ben asked.

"You probably weren't around three years ago when the FBI closed the case of the two murdered people in this county. I didn't think they had it right, but they dismissed what I had to say. The picture of the person who ordered my shooting is Charles Warren, who the FBI said had been killed and put in one of our watershed ponds. I had met him some years before the murders, and my gut feeling was that the body in the pond wasn't him. They found his wife's body in an underground cavern on Meadow Creek and declared that he and his wife had been murdered. As far as I know, there hasn't been anything new on the case since. It has gone unsolved. I will swear in court that the person in this picture is indeed Charles Warren, the deputy in Botetourt County who went missing, and you guys said was the body in the pond."

"The guys did say that whoever this man is, he mentioned he saw you in his hotel in the Keys and knew that if you saw him, you would know he wasn't dead, and he'd be on the run for the rest of his life."

"That makes sense. I'm glad the guy was a lousy shot."

"Me too," Ben said. "You need to have the case reopened and put out an APB for Charles Warren, last seen in the Keys in Florida."

"Yes, Clifford, I'll see that happens today when I get back to Roanoke. You'd better be careful; he might try to come after you if he thinks you're the only one who can make trouble for him."

"I'll take extra precautions for a while until we see what happens. Ben, keep me informed of whatever you find out. Sometimes this little county doesn't get informed of things as they should."

"No problem, Clifford."

Ben had no more than pulled out of the parking lot when Clifford's cell phone began ringing.

"Morning, Clifford Davidson speaking. How may I help you?"

"Hey, Cliff, this is John Elmore. I guess you've heard about the guys who shot at you and hit Joan."

"Yes. How is Joan?"

"She's just fine; there's just a small scar where the bullet entered and exited. I'm calling because we need you to come back down to the Keys as a witness to the shooting. You can identify the guys in the car, can't you?"

"Oh yes, I got a good look at them. When do you need me to come back down there?"

"Next Tuesday. We'll send you an airline ticket that will get you to Miami, and a state police helicopter will bring you down to the Keys. I shouldn't have a problem getting away for a day or two."

"I'll see you on Tuesday."

Tuesday arrived, and Clifford had already received his airline tickets. He had one of his deputies take him to the

Blacksburg/Roanoke Regional Airport. Four hours later, he walked out of the Miami airport, where an FBI agent met him and escorted him to a private fenced area. They boarded a helicopter, and within an hour, he was let out at the police station on Ballast Key Island. John Elmore met him there and took him to the same hotel where Janet and he had stayed.

"Get settled, and I'll pick you up later this evening around four o'clock. Joan and I will take you to dinner."

"That will be fine, as long as someone doesn't take a shot at us," Clifford joked, then smiled with a toothy grin.

Clifford enjoyed his dinner with John and Joan and was glad to see she was doing fine after the wound. The next day, he went to court and testified that these were the men in the Ford Mustang who had fired the shot that struck Joan Elmore.

The men would be sentenced on another date for their crime. Clifford said goodbye to the Elmores and made his way back to New Castle. Janet was relieved to have him back home; she had been uneasy about his return to Florida after the shooting incidents. She hoped the trouble would not follow them home to Craig County.

Chapter Nineteen

Things were quiet in the little town of New Castle for the next couple of months, with nothing but domestic disputes and speeding tickets. On weekends, a few public intoxication charges came up, but those were becoming rare.

Janet and the kids were doing fine, and he had not heard anything from Florida or the FBI concerning Charles Warren's whereabouts.

One pleasant day, he needed to go into Roanoke to look for supplies for the office. Since he had to be in the downtown area, he decided to have lunch at Paul's Restaurant.

The restaurant was packed when he arrived, but he found a spot at the bar and ordered their lunch special. He enjoyed his hoagie and coffee as some of the crowd cleared out and went back to work.

After finishing his lunch, he went up to the bar where the cash register was to pay his bill. Demos, the owner, was very friendly and thanked him for dining there.

As Clifford opened the door to leave, he had to wait for a man to enter the restaurant before he could exit. He recognized the man but didn't let on.

Instead, he said, "Excuse me," let him in, and then continued out and down the street. He called the FBI immediately.

A new voice answered the phone: "Captain George here, may I help you?"

Clifford went through all the preliminaries and informed him about seeing Charles Warren entering the restaurant. Captain George, aware of the case, said that their office was only a block away and that he would have two agents on the scene within five minutes. Sure enough, two FBI agents arrived running up the street. Clifford flagged them down and briefed them on what he had seen.

"I can go in first and point him out if that will make it easier for you to arrest the right person," he offered. They agreed, and the three men went inside, with Clifford leading. He walked past where Charles Warren was sitting, then turned and indicated to the agents the man he had seen.

The agents approached Warren, drew their weapons, and instructed him to get up slowly and turn around. He complied, and they cuffed him and checked him for any weapons. Finding him unarmed, they walked him out of the restaurant, with Clifford following. Warren stared at Clifford and remarked, "I knew you would be trouble the first time I saw you and your deputy in that restaurant in Craig County."

Charles Warren admitted to murdering his wife in a jealous rage after catching her with a boyfriend. He had shot both of them and then decided to dispose of their bodies in separate locations. To cover his tracks, he removed any paperwork linking him to Botetourt and erased traces of his employment with the Botetourt Sheriff's Office. He was surprised that both bodies had been discovered so quickly.

THE MORAL OF THIS STORY IS:

IF YOU DO THE CRIME, YOU DO THE TIME. Charles Warren is now serving two life sentences with no possibility of parole.

The End

Look for Book Four, The Mine, coming soon

Milton Keynes UK
Ingram Content Group UK Ltd.
UKHW021526301124
451951UK00004B/22